BY F. SCOTT FITZGERALD

NOVELS

The Love of the Last Tycoon *(unfinished)*
Tender Is the Night
The Great Gatsby
The Beautiful and Damned
This Side of Paradise

STORIES

Bits of Paradise
The Basil and Josephine Stories
The Pat Hobby Stories
Taps at Reveille
Six Tales of the Jazz Age and Other Stories
Flappers and Philosophers
The Stories of F. Scott Fitzgerald
Babylon Revisited and Other Stories
The Short Stories of F. Scott Fitzgerald

STORIES AND ESSAYS

Afternoon of an Author
The Fitzgerald Reader

LETTERS

A Life in Letters
The Letters of F. Scott Fitzgerald
Letters to His Daughter
Dear Scott/Dear Max

AND A COMEDY

The Vegetable

The Curious Case Of
BENJAMIN BUTTON

STORY TO SCREENPLAY

STORY BY

F. Scott Fitzgerald

SCREENPLAY BY

Eric Roth

SCREEN STORY BY

Eric Roth

AND

Robin Swicord

SCRIBNER

New York London Toronto Sydney

SCRIBNER
A Division of Simon & Schuster, Inc.
1230 Avenue of the Americas
New York, NY 10020

This Scribner trade paperback edition December 2008

For information about special discounts for bulk purchases,
please contact Simon & Schuster Special Sales:
1-800-456-6798 or business@simonandschuster.com.

Text set in Stempel Garamond

Manufactured in the United States of America

5   7   9   10   8   6   4

Library of Congress Control Number: 2007280415

ISBN-13: 978-1-4391-1700-2
ISBN-10: 1-4391-1700-4

The Curious Case Of
BENJAMIN BUTTON

THE CURIOUS CASE
OF BENJAMIN BUTTON

As long ago as 1860 it was the proper thing to be born at home. At present, so I am told, the high gods of medicine have decreed that the first cries of the young shall be uttered upon the anesthetic air of a hospital, preferably a fashionable one. So young Mr. and Mrs. Roger Button were fifty years ahead of style when they decided, one day in the summer of 1860, that their first baby should be born in a hospital. Whether this anachronism had any bearing upon the astonishing history I am about to set down will never be known.

I shall tell you what occurred, and let you judge for yourself.

The Roger Buttons held an enviable position, both social and financial, in ante-bellum Baltimore. They were related to the This Family and the That Family, which, as every Southerner knew, entitled them to membership in that enormous peerage which largely populated the Confederacy. This was their first experience with the charming old custom of having babies—Mr. Button was naturally nervous. He hoped it would be a boy so that he could be sent to Yale College in Connecticut, at which institution Mr. Button himself had been known for four years by the somewhat obvious nickname of "Cuff."

On the September morning consecrated to the enormous event he arose nervously at six o'clock, dressed himself, adjusted an impeccable stock, and hurried forth through the streets of Baltimore to the hospital, to determine whether the darkness of the night had borne in new life upon its bosom.

When he was approximately a hundred yards from the Maryland Private Hospital for Ladies and Gentlemen he saw Doctor Keene, the family physician, descending the front steps, rubbing his hands together with a washing movement—as all doctors are required to do by the unwritten ethics of their profession.

Mr. Roger Button, the president of Roger Button & Co., Wholesale Hardware, began to run toward Doctor Keene with much less dignity than was expected from a Southern gentleman of that picturesque period. "Doctor Keene!" he called. "Oh, Doctor Keene!"

The doctor heard him, faced around, and stood waiting, a curious expression settling on his harsh, medicinal face as Mr. Button drew near.

"What happened?" demanded Mr. Button, as he came up in a gasping rush. "What was it? How is she? A boy? Who is it? What—"

"Talk sense!" said Doctor Keene sharply. He appeared somewhat irritated.

"Is the child born?" begged Mr. Button.

Doctor Keene frowned. "Why, yes, I suppose so—after a fashion." Again he threw a curious glance at Mr. Button.

"Is my wife all right?"

"Yes."

"Is it a boy or a girl?"

"Here now!" cried Doctor Keene in a perfect passion of irritation, "I'll ask you to go and see for yourself. Outrageous!" He snapped the last word out in almost one syllable, then he turned away muttering: "Do you imagine a case like this will help my professional reputation? One more would ruin me—ruin anybody."

"What's the matter?" demanded Mr. Button, appalled. "Triplets?"

"No, not triplets!" answered the doctor cuttingly. "What's more, you can go and see for yourself. And get another doctor. I brought you into the world, young man, and I've been physician to your family for forty years, but I'm through with you! I don't want to see you or any of your relatives ever again! Good-bye!"

Then he turned sharply, and without another word climbed into his phaeton, which was waiting at the curbstone, and drove severely away.

Mr. Button stood there upon the sidewalk, stupefied and trembling from head to foot. What horrible mishap had occurred? He had suddenly lost all desire to go into the Maryland Private Hospital for Ladies and Gentlemen—it was with the greatest difficulty that, a moment later, he forced himself to mount the steps and enter the front door.

A nurse was sitting behind a desk in the opaque gloom of the hall. Swallowing his shame, Mr. Button approached her.

"Good-morning," she remarked, looking up at him pleasantly.

"Good-morning. I—I am Mr. Button."

At this a look of utter terror spread itself over the girl's face. She rose to her feet and seemed about to fly from the hall, restraining herself only with the most apparent difficulty.

"I want to see my child," said Mr. Button.

The nurse gave a little scream. "Oh—of course!" she cried hysterically. "Upstairs. Right upstairs. Go—*up*!"

She pointed the direction, and Mr. Button, bathed in a cool perspiration, turned falteringly, and began to mount to the second floor. In the upper hall he addressed another nurse who approached him, basin in hand. "I'm Mr. Button," he managed to articulate. "I want to see my—"

Clank! The basin clattered to the floor and rolled in the direction of the stairs. Clank! Clank! It began a methodical descent as if sharing in the general terror which this gentleman provoked.

"I want to see my child!" Mr. Button almost shrieked. He was on the verge of collapse.

Clank! The basin had reached the first floor. The nurse regained control of herself, and threw Mr. Button a look of hearty contempt.

"All *right*, Mr. Button," she agreed in a hushed voice. "Very *well*! But if you *knew* what state it's put us all in this morning! It's perfectly outrageous! The hospital will never have the ghost of a reputation after—"

"Hurry!" he cried hoarsely. "I can't stand this!"

"Come this way, then, Mr. Button."

He dragged himself after her. At the end of a long hall they reached a room from which proceeded a variety of howls—indeed, a room which, in later parlance, would have been known as the "crying-room." They entered. Ranged around the walls were half a dozen white-enameled rolling cribs, each with a tag tied at the head.

"Well," gasped Mr. Button, "which is mine?"

"There!" said the nurse.

Mr. Button's eyes followed her pointing finger, and this is what he saw. Wrapped in a voluminous white blanket, and partially crammed into one of the cribs, there sat an old man apparently about seventy years of age. His sparse hair was almost white, and from his chin dripped a long smoke-colored beard, which waved absurdly back and forth, fanned by the breeze coming in at the window. He looked up at Mr. Button with dim, faded eyes in which lurked a puzzled question.

"Am I mad?" thundered Mr. Button, his terror resolving into rage. "Is this some ghastly hospital joke?"

"It doesn't seem like a joke to us," replied the nurse severely. "And I don't know whether you're mad or not—but that is most certainly your child."

The cool perspiration redoubled on Mr. Button's forehead. He closed his eyes, and then, opening them, looked again. There was no mistake—he was gazing at a man of threescore and ten—a *baby* of threescore and ten, a baby whose feet hung over the sides of the crib in which it was reposing.

The old man looked placidly from one to the other for a moment, and then suddenly spoke in a cracked and ancient voice. "Are you my father?" he demanded.

Mr. Button and the nurse started violently.

"Because if you are," went on the old man querulously, "I wish you'd get me out of this place—or, at least, get them to put a comfortable rocker in here."

"Where in God's name did you come from? Who are you?" burst out Mr. Button frantically.

"I can't tell you *exactly* who I am," replied the querulous whine, "because I've only been born a few hours—but my last name is certainly Button."

"You lie! You're an impostor!"

The old man turned wearily to the nurse. "Nice way to welcome a newborn child," he complained in a weak voice. "Tell him he's wrong, why don't you?"

"You're wrong, Mr. Button," said the nurse severely. "This is your child, and you'll have to make the best of it. We're going to ask you to take him home with you as soon as possible—some time today."

"Home?" repeated Mr. Button incredulously.

"Yes, we can't have him here. We really can't, you know?"

"I'm right glad of it," whined the old man. "This is a fine place to keep a youngster of quiet tastes. With all this yelling and howling, I haven't been able to get a wink of sleep. I asked for something to eat"—here his voice rose to a shrill note of protest—"and they brought me a bottle of milk!"

Mr. Button sank down upon a chair near his son and concealed his face in his hands. "My heavens!" he murmured, in an ecstasy of horror. "What will people say? What must I do?"

"You'll have to take him home," insisted the nurse—"immediately!"

A grotesque picture formed itself with dreadful clarity before the eyes of the tortured man—a picture of himself walking through the crowded streets of the city with this appalling apparition stalking by his side. "I can't. I can't," he moaned.

People would stop to speak to him, and what was he going to say? He would have to introduce this—this septuagenarian: "This is my son, born early this morning." And then the old man would gather his blanket around him and they would plod on, past the bustling stores, the slave market—for a dark instant Mr. Button wished passionately that his son was black—past the luxurious houses of the residential district, past the home for the aged. . . .

"Come! Pull yourself together," commanded the nurse.

"See here," the old man announced suddenly, "if you think I'm going to walk home in this blanket, you're entirely mistaken."

"Babies always have blankets."

With a malicious crackle the old man held up a small white swaddling garment. "Look!" he quavered. "*This* is what they had ready for me."

"Babies always wear those," said the nurse primly.

"Well," said the old man, "this baby's not going to wear anything in about two minutes. This blanket itches. They might at least have given me a sheet."

"Keep it on! Keep it on!" said Mr. Button hurriedly. He turned to the nurse. "What'll I do?"

"Go downtown and buy your son some clothes."

Mr. Button's son's voice followed him down into the hall: "And a cane, father. I want to have a cane."

Mr. Button banged the outer door savagely. . . .

II

"Good-morning," Mr. Button said, nervously, to the clerk in the Chesapeake Dry Goods Company. "I want to buy some clothes for my child."

"How old is your child, sir?"

"About six hours," answered Mr. Button, without due consideration.

"Babies' supply department in the rear."

"Why, I don't think—I'm not sure that's what I want. It's—he's an unusually large-size child. Exceptionally—ah—large."

"They have the largest child's sizes."

"Where is the boys' department?" inquired Mr. Button, shifting his ground desperately. He felt that the clerk must surely scent his shameful secret.

"Right here."

"Well—" He hesitated. The notion of dressing his son in men's clothes was repugnant to him. If, say, he could only find a *very* large boy's suit, he might cut off that long and awful beard, dye the white hair brown, and thus manage to conceal the worst, and to retain something of his own self-respect—not to mention his position in Baltimore society.

But a frantic inspection of the boys' department revealed no suits to fit the new-born Button. He blamed the store, of course—in such cases it is the thing to blame the store.

"How old did you say that boy of yours was?" demanded the clerk curiously.

"He's—sixteen."

"Oh, I beg your pardon. I thought you said six *hours.* You'll find the youths' department in the next aisle."

Mr. Button turned miserably away. Then he stopped, brightened, and pointed his finger toward a dressed dummy in the window display. "There!" he exclaimed. "I'll take that suit, out there on the dummy."

The clerk stared. "Why," he protested, "that's not a child's suit. At least it *is*, but it's for fancy dress. You could wear it yourself!"

"Wrap it up," insisted his customer nervously. "That's what I want."

The astonished clerk obeyed.

Back at the hospital Mr. Button entered the nursery and almost threw the package at his son. "Here's your clothes," he snapped out.

The old man untied the package and viewed the contents with a quizzical eye.

"They look sort of funny to me," he complained. "I don't want to be made a monkey of —"

"You've made a monkey of me!" retorted Mr. Button fiercely. "Never you mind how funny you look. Put them on — or I'll — or I'll *spank* you." He swallowed uneasily at the penultimate word, feeling nevertheless that it was the proper thing to say.

"All right, father" — this with a grotesque simulation of filial respect — "you've lived longer; you know best. Just as you say."

As before, the sound of the word "father" caused Mr. Button to start violently.

"And hurry."

"I'm hurrying, father."

When his son was dressed Mr. Button regarded him with depression. The costume consisted of dotted socks, pink pants, and a belted blouse with a wide white collar. Over the latter waved the long whitish beard, drooping almost to the waist. The effect was not good.

"Wait!"

Mr. Button seized a hospital shears and with three quick snaps amputated a large section of the beard. But even with this improvement the ensemble fell far short of perfection. The remaining brush of scraggly hair, the watery eyes, the ancient teeth, seemed oddly out of tone with the gayety of the costume. Mr. Button, however, was obdurate—he held out his hand. "Come along!" he said sternly.

His son took the hand trustingly. "What are you going to call me, dad?" he quavered as they walked from the nursery—"just 'baby' for a while? till you think of a better name?"

Mr. Button grunted. "I don't know," he answered harshly. "I think we'll call you Methuselah."

III

Even after the new addition to the Button family had had his hair cut short and then dyed to a sparse unnatural black, had had his face shaved so close that it glistened, and had been attired in small-boy clothes made to order by a flabbergasted tailor, it was impossible for Mr. Button to ignore the fact that his son was a poor excuse for a first family baby. Despite his aged stoop, Benjamin Button—for it was by this name they called him instead of by the appropriate but invidious Methuselah—was five feet eight inches tall. His clothes did not conceal this, nor did the clipping and dyeing of his eyebrows disguise the fact that the eyes underneath were faded and watery and tired. In fact, the baby-nurse who had been engaged in advance left the house after one look, in a state of considerable indignation.

But Mr. Button persisted in his unwavering purpose. Benjamin was a baby, and a baby he should remain. At first he declared that if Benjamin didn't like warm milk he could go without food altogether, but he was finally prevailed upon to allow his son bread and butter, and even oatmeal by way of a compromise. One day he brought home a rattle and, giving it to Benjamin, insisted in no uncertain terms that he should "play with it," whereupon the old man took it with a weary expression and could be heard jingling it obediently at intervals throughout the day.

There can be no doubt, though, that the rattle bored him, and that he found other and more soothing amusements when he was left alone. For instance, Mr. Button discovered one day that during the preceding week he had smoked more cigars than ever before—a phenomenon which was explained a few days later when, entering the nursery unexpectedly, he found the room full of faint blue haze and Benjamin, with a guilty expression on his face, trying to conceal the butt of a dark Havana. This, of course, called for a severe spanking, but Mr. Button found that he could not bring himself to administer it. He merely warned his son that he would "stunt his growth."

Nevertheless he persisted in his attitude. He brought home lead soldiers, he brought toy trains, he brought large pleasant animals made of cotton, and, to perfect the illusion which he was creating—for himself at least—he passionately demanded of the clerk in the toy-store whether "the paint would come off the pink duck if the baby put it in his mouth." But, despite all his father's efforts, Benjamin refused to be interested. He would steal down the back stairs and return to the nursery with a volume of the "Encyclopædia Britannica," over which he would pore through an afternoon, while his cotton cows and his Noah's ark were left neglected on the floor. Against such a stubbornness Mr. Button's efforts were of little avail.

The sensation created in Baltimore was, at first, prodigious. What the mishap would have cost the Buttons and their kinsfolk socially cannot be determined, for the outbreak of the Civil War drew the city's attention to other things. A few people who were unfailingly polite racked their brains for compliments to give to the parents— and finally hit upon the ingenious device of declaring that the baby resembled his grandfather, a fact which, due to the standard state of decay common to all men of seventy, could not be denied. Mr. and

Mrs. Roger Button were not pleased, and Benjamin's grandfather was furiously insulted.

Benjamin, once he left the hospital, took life as he found it. Several small boys were brought to see him, and he spent a stiff-jointed afternoon trying to work up an interest in tops and marbles—he even managed, quite accidentally, to break a kitchen window with a stone from a sling shot, a feat which secretly delighted his father.

Thereafter Benjamin contrived to break something every day, but he did these things only because they were expected of him, and because he was by nature obliging.

When his grandfather's initial antagonism wore off, Benjamin and that gentleman took enormous pleasure in one another's company. They would sit for hours, these two so far apart in age and experience, and, like old cronies, discuss with tireless monotony the slow events of the day. Benjamin felt more at ease in his grandfather's presence than in his parents'—they seemed always somewhat in awe of him and, despite the dictatorial authority they exercised over him, frequently addressed him as "Mr."

He was as puzzled as anyone else at the apparently advanced age of his mind and body at birth. He read up on it in the medical journal, but found that no such case had been previously recorded. At his father's urging he made an honest attempt to play with other boys, and frequently he joined in the milder games—football shook him up too much, and he feared that in case of a fracture his ancient bones would refuse to knit.

When he was five he was sent to kindergarten, where he was initiated into the art of pasting green paper on orange paper, of weaving colored maps and manufacturing eternal cardboard necklaces. He was inclined to drowse off to sleep in the middle of these tasks, a habit which both irritated and frightened his young teacher. To his relief she complained to his parents, and he was removed from the school. The Roger Buttons told their friends that they felt he was too young.

By the time he was twelve years old his parents had grown used to him. Indeed, so strong is the force of custom that they no longer felt that he was different from any other child—except when some curious anomaly reminded them of the fact. But one day a few weeks after his twelfth birthday, while looking in the mirror, Benjamin made, or thought he made, an astonishing discovery. Did his eyes deceive him, or had his hair turned in the dozen years of his life from white to iron-gray under its concealing dye? Was the network of wrinkles on his face becoming less pronounced? Was his skin healthier and firmer, with even a touch of ruddy winter color? He could not tell. He knew that he no longer stooped and that his physical condition had improved since the early days of his life.

"Can it be—?" he thought to himself, or, rather, scarcely dared to think.

He went to his father. "I am grown," he announced determinedly. "I want to put on long trousers."

His father hesitated. "Well," he said finally, "I don't know. Fourteen is the age for putting on long trousers—and you are only twelve."

"But you'll have to admit," protested Benjamin, "that I'm big for my age."

His father looked at him with illusory speculation. "Oh, I'm not so sure of that," he said. "I was as big as you when I was twelve."

This was not true—it was all part of Roger Button's silent agreement with himself to believe in his son's normality.

Finally a compromise was reached. Benjamin was to continue to dye his hair. He was to make a better attempt to play with boys of his own age. He was not to wear his spectacles or carry a cane in the street. In return for these concessions he was allowed his first suit of long trousers. . . .

IV

Of the life of Benjamin Button between his twelfth and twenty-first year I intend to say little. Suffice to record that they were years of normal ungrowth. When Benjamin was eighteen he was erect as a man of fifty; he had more hair and it was of a dark gray; his step was firm, his voice had lost its cracked quaver and descended to a healthy baritone. So his father sent him up to Connecticut to take examinations for entrance to Yale College. Benjamin passed his examination and became a member of the freshman class.

On the third day following his matriculation he received a notification from Mr. Hart, the college registrar, to call at his office and arrange his schedule. Benjamin, glancing in the mirror, decided that his hair needed a new application of its brown dye, but an anxious inspection of his bureau drawer disclosed that the dye bottle was not there. Then he remembered—he had emptied it the day before and thrown it away.

He was in a dilemma. He was due at the registrar's in five minutes. There seemed to be no help for it—he must go as he was. He did.

"Good-morning," said the registrar politely. "You've come to inquire about your son."

"Why, as a matter of fact, my name's Button—" began Benjamin, but Mr. Hart cut him off.

"I'm very glad to meet you, Mr. Button. I'm expecting your son here any minute."

"That's me!" burst out Benjamin. "I'm a freshman."

"What!"

"I'm a freshman."

"Surely you're joking."

"Not at all."

The registrar frowned and glanced at a card before him. "Why, I have Mr. Benjamin Button's age down here as eighteen."

"That's my age," asserted Benjamin, flushing slightly.

The registrar eyed him wearily. "Now surely, Mr. Button, you don't expect me to believe that."

Benjamin smiled wearily. "I am eighteen," he repeated.

The registrar pointed sternly to the door. "Get out," he said. "Get out of college and get out of town. You are a dangerous lunatic."

"I am eighteen."

Mr. Hart opened the door. "The idea!" he shouted. "A man of your age trying to enter here as a freshman. Eighteen years old, are you? Well, I'll give you eighteen minutes to get out of town."

Benjamin Button walked with dignity from the room, and half a dozen undergraduates, who were waiting in the hall, followed him curiously with their eyes. When he had gone a little way he turned around, faced the infuriated registrar, who was still standing in the doorway, and repeated in a firm voice: "I am eighteen years old."

To a chorus of titters which went up from the group of under-graduates, Benjamin walked away.

But he was not fated to escape so easily. On his melancholy walk to the railroad station he found that he was being followed by a group, then by a swarm, and finally by a dense mass of undergrad-uates. The word had gone around that a lunatic had passed the entrance examinations for Yale and attempted to palm himself off as a youth of eighteen. A fever of excitement permeated the college. Men ran hatless out of classes, the football team abandoned its practice and joined the mob, professors' wives with bonnets awry and bustles out of position, ran shouting after the procession, from which proceeded a continual succession of remarks aimed at the tender sensibilities of Benjamin Button.

"He must be the Wandering Jew!"

"He ought to go to prep school at his age!"

"Look at the infant prodigy!"

"He thought this was the old men's home."

"Go up to Harvard!"

Benjamin increased his gait, and soon he was running. He would show them! He *would* go to Harvard, and then they would regret these ill-considered taunts!

Safely on board the train for Baltimore, he put his head from the window. "You'll regret this!" he shouted.

"Ha-ha!" the undergraduates laughed. "Ha-ha-ha!" It was the biggest mistake that Yale College had ever made. . . .

V

In 1880 Benjamin Button was twenty years old, and he signalized his birthday by going to work for his father in Roger Button & Co., Wholesale Hardware. It was in that same year that he began "going out socially"—that is, his father insisted on taking him to several fashionable dances. Roger Button was now fifty, and he and his son were more and more companionable—in fact, since Benjamin had ceased to dye his hair (which was still grayish) they appeared about the same age, and could have passed for brothers.

One night in August they got into the phaeton attired in their full-dress suits and drove out to a dance at the Shevlins' country house, situated just outside of Baltimore. It was a gorgeous evening. A full moon drenched the road to the lustreless color of platinum, and late-blooming harvest flowers breathed into the motionless air aromas that were like low, half-heard laughter. The open country, carpeted for rods around with bright wheat, was translucent as in the day. It was almost impossible not to be affected by the sheer beauty of the sky—almost.

"There's a great future in the dry-goods business," Roger Button was saying. He was not a spiritual man—his esthetic sense was rudimentary.

"Old fellows like me can't learn new tricks," he observed profoundly. "It's you youngsters with energy and vitality that have the great future before you."

Far up the road the lights of the Shevlins' country house drifted into view, and presently there was a sighing sound that crept persistently toward them—it might have been the fine plaint of violins or the rustle of the silver wheat under the moon.

They pulled up behind a handsome brougham whose passengers were disembarking at the door. A lady got out, then an elderly gentleman, then another young lady, beautiful as sin. Benjamin started; an almost chemical change seemed to dissolve and recompose the very elements of his body. A rigor passed over him, blood rose into his cheeks, his forehead, and there was a steady thumping in his ears. It was first love.

The girl was slender and frail, with hair that was ashen under the moon and honey-colored under the sputtering gas-lamps of the porch. Over her shoulders was thrown a Spanish mantilla of softest yellow, butterflied in black; her feet were glittering buttons at the hem of her bustled dress.

Roger Button leaned over to his son. "That," he said, "is young Hildegarde Moncrief, the daughter of General Moncrief."

Benjamin nodded coldly. "Pretty little thing," he said indifferently. But when the negro boy had led the buggy away, he added: "Dad, you might introduce me to her."

They approached a group of which Miss Moncrief was the center. Reared in the old tradition, she courtesied low before Benjamin. Yes, he might have a dance. He thanked her and walked away—staggered away.

The interval until the time for his turn should arrive dragged itself out interminably. He stood close to the wall, silent, inscrutable, watching with murderous eyes the young bloods of Baltimore as they eddied around Hildegarde Moncrief, passionate admiration in their faces. How obnoxious they seemed to Benjamin; how intolerably rosy! Their curling brown whiskers aroused in him a feeling equivalent to indigestion.

But when his own time came, and he drifted with her out upon the changing floor to the music of the latest waltz from Paris, his jealousies and anxieties melted from him like a mantle of snow. Blind with enchantment, he felt that life was just beginning.

"You and your brother got here just as we did, didn't you?" asked Hildegarde, looking up at him with eyes that were like bright blue enamel.

Benjamin hesitated. If she took him for his father's brother, would it be best to enlighten her? He remembered his experience at Yale, so he decided against it. It would be rude to contradict a lady; it would be criminal to mar this exquisite occasion with the grotesque story of his origin. Later, perhaps. So he nodded, smiled, listened, was happy.

"I like men of your age," Hildegarde told him. "Young boys are so idiotic. They tell me how much champagne they drink at college, and how much money they lose playing cards. Men of your age know how to appreciate women."

Benjamin felt himself on the verge of a proposal—with an effort he choked back the impulse.

"You're just the romantic age," she continued—"fifty. Twenty-five is too worldly-wise; thirty is apt to be pale from overwork; forty is the age of long stories that take a whole cigar to tell; sixty is—oh, sixty is too near seventy; but fifty is the mellow age. I love fifty."

Fifty seemed to Benjamin a glorious age. He longed passionately to be fifty.

"I've always said," went on Hildegarde, "that I'd rather marry a man of fifty and be taken care of than marry a man of thirty and take care of *him.*"

For Benjamin the rest of the evening was bathed in a honey-colored mist. Hildegarde gave him two more dances, and they discovered that they were marvellously in accord on all the questions of the day. She was to go driving with him on the following Sunday, and then they would discuss all these questions further.

Going home in the phaeton just before the crack of dawn, when the first bees were humming and the fading moon glimmered in the cool dew, Benjamin knew vaguely that his father was discussing wholesale hardware.

". . . And what do you think should merit our biggest attention after hammers and nails?" the elder Button was saying.

"Love," replied Benjamin absent-mindedly.

"Lugs?" exclaimed Roger Button. "Why, I've just covered the question of lugs."

Benjamin regarded him with dazed eyes just as the eastern sky was suddenly cracked with light, and an oriole yawned piercingly in the quickening trees. . . .

VI

When, six months later, the engagement of Miss Hildegarde Moncrief to Mr. Benjamin Button was made known (I say "made known," for General Moncrief declared he would rather fall upon his sword than announce it), the excitement in Baltimore society reached a feverish pitch. The almost forgotten story of Benjamin's birth was remembered and sent out upon the winds of scandal in picaresque and incredible forms. It was said that Benjamin was really the father of Roger Button, that he was his brother who had been in prison for forty years, that he was John Wilkes Booth in disguise—and, finally, that he had two small conical horns sprouting from his head.

The Sunday supplements of the New York papers played up the case with fascinating sketches which showed the head of Benjamin Button attached to a fish, to a snake, and, finally, to a body of solid brass. He became known, journalistically, as the Mystery Man of Maryland. But the true story, as is usually the case, had a very small circulation.

However, everyone agreed with General Moncrief that it was "criminal" for a lovely girl who could have married any beau in Baltimore to throw herself into the arms of a man who was assuredly fifty. In vain Mr. Roger Button published his son's birth certificate in large type in the Baltimore *Blaze.* No one believed it. You had only to look at Benjamin and see.

On the part of the two people most concerned there was no wavering. So many of the stories about her fiancé were false that Hildegarde refused stubbornly to believe even the true one. In vain General Moncrief pointed out to her the high mortality among men of fifty—or, at least, among men who looked fifty; in vain he told her of the instability of the wholesale hardware business. Hildegarde had chosen to marry for mellowness—and marry she did. . . .

VII

In one particular, at least, the friends of Hildegarde Moncrief were mistaken. The wholesale hardware business prospered amazingly. In the fifteen years between Benjamin Button's marriage in 1880 and his father's retirement in 1895, the family fortune was doubled—and this was due largely to the younger member of the firm.

Needless to say, Baltimore eventually received the couple to its bosom. Even old General Moncrief became reconciled to his son-in-law when Benjamin gave him the money to bring out his "History of the Civil War" in twenty volumes, which had been refused by nine prominent publishers.

In Benjamin himself fifteen years had wrought many changes. It seemed to him that the blood flowed with new vigor through his veins. It began to be a pleasure to rise in the morning, to walk with an active step along the busy, sunny street, to work untiringly with his shipments of hammers and his cargoes of nails. It was in 1890 that he executed his famous business coup: he brought up the suggestion that *all nails used in nailing up the boxes in which nails are shipped are the property of the shippee,* a proposal which became a statute, was approved by Chief Justice Fossile, and saved Roger Button & Company, Wholesale Hardware, more than *six hundred nails every year.*

In addition, Benjamin discovered that he was becoming more and more attracted by the gay side of life. It was typical of his growing enthusiasm for pleasure that he was the first man in the city of Baltimore to own and run an automobile. Meeting him on the street, his contemporaries would stare enviously at the picture he made of health and vitality.

"He seems to grow younger every year," they would remark. And if old Roger Button, now sixty-five years old, had failed at first to give a proper welcome to his son he atoned at last by bestowing on him what amounted to adulation.

And here we come to an unpleasant subject which it will be well to pass over as quickly as possible. There was only one thing that worried Benjamin Button: his wife had ceased to attract him.

At that time Hildegarde was a woman of thirty-five, with a son, Roscoe, fourteen years old. In the early days of their marriage Benjamin had worshipped her. But, as the years passed, her honey-colored hair became an unexciting brown, the blue enamel of her eyes assumed the aspect of cheap crockery—moreover, and most of all, she had become too settled in her ways, too placid, too content, too anemic in her excitements, and too sober in her taste. As a bride it had been she who had "dragged" Benjamin to dances and dinners—now conditions were reversed. She went out socially with him, but without enthusiasm, devoured already by that eternal inertia which comes to live with each of us one day and stays with us to the end.

Benjamin's discontent waxed stronger. At the outbreak of the Spanish-American War in 1898 his home had for him so little charm that he decided to join the army. With his business influence he obtained a commission as captain, and proved so adaptable to the work that he was made a major, and finally a lieutenant-colonel just in time to participate in the celebrated charge up San Juan Hill. He was slightly wounded, and received a medal.

Benjamin had become so attached to the activity and excitement of army life that he regretted to give it up, but his business required attention, so he resigned his commission and came home. He was met at the station by a brass band and escorted to his house.

VIII

Hildegarde, waving a large silk flag, greeted him on the porch, and even as he kissed her he felt with a sinking of the heart that these three years had taken their toll. She was a woman of forty now, with a faint skirmish line of gray hairs in her head. The sight depressed him.

Up in his room he saw his reflection in the familiar mirror—he went closer and examined his own face with anxiety, comparing it after a moment with a photograph of himself in uniform taken just before the war.

"Good Lord!" he said aloud. The process was continuing. There was no doubt of it—he looked now like a man of thirty. Instead of being delighted, he was uneasy—he was growing younger. He had hitherto hoped that once he reached a bodily age equivalent to his age in years, the grotesque phenomenon which had marked his birth would cease to function. He shuddered. His destiny seemed to him awful, incredible.

When he came downstairs Hildegarde was waiting for him. She appeared annoyed, and he wondered if she had at last discovered that there was something amiss. It was with an effort to relieve the tension between them that he broached the matter at dinner in what he considered a delicate way.

"Well," he remarked lightly, "everybody says I look younger than ever."

Hildegarde regarded him with scorn. She sniffed. "Do you think it's anything to boast about?"

"I'm not boasting," he asserted uncomfortably.

She sniffed again. "The idea," she said, and after a moment: "I should think you'd have enough pride to stop it."

"How can I?" he demanded.

"I'm not going to argue with you," she retorted. "But there's a right way of doing things and a wrong way. If you've made up your mind to be different from everybody else, I don't suppose I can stop you, but I really don't think it's very considerate."

"But, Hildegarde, I can't help it."

"You can too. You're simply stubborn. You think you don't want to be like any one else. You always have been that way, and you always will be. But just think how it would be if every one else looked at things as you do—what would the world be like?"

As this was an inane and unanswerable argument Benjamin made no reply, and from that time on a chasm began to widen between them. He wondered what possible fascination she had ever exercised over him.

To add to the breach, he found, as the new century gathered headway, that his thirst for gayety grew stronger. Never a party of any kind in the city of Baltimore but he was there, dancing with the prettiest of the young married women, chatting with the most popular of the débutantes, and finding their company charming, while his wife, a dowager of evil omen, sat among the chaperons, now in haughty disapproval, and now following him with solemn, puzzled, and reproachful eyes.

"Look!" people would remark. "What a pity! A young fellow that age tied to a woman of forty-five. He must be twenty years younger than his wife." They had forgotten—as people inevitably forget—that back in 1880 their mammas and papas had also remarked about this same ill-matched pair.

Benjamin's growing unhappiness at home was compensated for by his many new interests. He took up golf and made a great success of it. He went in for dancing: in 1906 he was an expert at "The Boston," and in 1908 he was considered proficient at the "Maxixe," while in 1909 his "Castle Walk" was the envy of every young man in town.

His social activities, of course, interfered to some extent with his business, but then he had worked hard at wholesale hardware for twenty-five years and felt that he could soon hand it on to his son, Roscoe, who had recently graduated from Harvard.

He and his son were, in fact, often mistaken for each other. This pleased Benjamin—he soon forgot the insidious fear which had come over him on his return from the Spanish-American War, and grew to take a naïve pleasure in his appearance. There was only one fly in the delicious ointment—he hated to appear in public with his wife. Hildegarde was almost fifty, and the sight of her made him feel absurd. . . .

IX

One September day in 1910—a few years after Roger Button & Co., Wholesale Hardware, had been handed over to young Roscoe Button—a man, apparently about twenty years old, entered himself as a freshman at Harvard University in Cambridge. He did not make the mistake of announcing that he would never see fifty again nor did he mention the fact that his son had been graduated from the same institution ten years before.

He was admitted, and almost immediately attained a prominent position in the class, partly because he seemed a little older than the other freshmen, whose average age was about eighteen.

But his success was largely due to the fact that in the football game with Yale he played so brilliantly, with so much dash and with such a cold, remorseless anger that he scored seven touchdowns and fourteen field goals for Harvard, and caused one entire eleven of Yale men to be carried singly from the field, unconscious. He was the most celebrated man in college.

Strange to say, in his third or junior year he was scarcely able to "make" the team. The coaches said that he had lost weight, and it seemed to the more observant among them that he was not quite as tall as before. He made no touchdowns—indeed, he was retained on the team chiefly in hope that his enormous reputation would bring terror and disorganization to the Yale team.

In his senior year he did not make the team at all. He had grown so slight and frail that one day he was taken by some sophomores for a freshman, an incident which humiliated him terribly. He became known as something of a prodigy—a senior who was surely no more than sixteen—and he was often shocked at the worldliness of some of his classmates. His studies seemed harder to him—he felt that they were too advanced. He had heard his classmates speak of

St. Midas', the famous preparatory school, at which so many of them had prepared for college, and he determined after his graduation to enter himself at St. Midas', where the sheltered life among boys his own size would be more congenial to him.

Upon his graduation in 1914 he went home to Baltimore with his Harvard diploma in his pocket. Hildegarde was now residing in Italy, so Benjamin went to live with his son, Roscoe. But though he was welcomed in a general way, there was obviously no heartiness in Roscoe's feeling toward him—there was even perceptible a tendency on his son's part to think that Benjamin, as he moped about the house in adolescent mooniness, was somewhat in the way. Roscoe was married now and prominent in Baltimore life, and he wanted no scandal to creep out in connection with his family.

Benjamin, no longer persona grata with the débutantes and younger college set, found himself left much alone, except for the companionship of three or four fifteen-year-old boys in the neighborhood. His idea of going to St. Midas' School recurred to him.

"Say," he said to Roscoe one day, "I've told you over and over that I want to go to prep school."

"Well, go, then," replied Roscoe shortly. The matter was distasteful to him, and he wished to avoid a discussion.

"I can't go alone," said Benjamin helplessly. "You'll have to enter me and take me up there."

"I haven't got time," declared Roscoe abruptly. His eyes narrowed and he looked uneasily at his father. "As a matter of fact," he added, "you'd better not go on with this business much longer. You better pull up short. You better—you better"—he paused and his face crimsoned as he sought for words—"you better turn right around and start back the other way. This has gone too far to be a joke. It isn't funny any longer. You—you behave yourself!"

Benjamin looked at him, on the verge of tears.

"And another thing," continued Roscoe, "when visitors are in the house I want you to call me 'Uncle'—not 'Roscoe,' but 'Uncle,' do you understand? It looks absurd for a boy of fifteen to call me by my first name. Perhaps you'd better call me 'Uncle' *all* the time, so you'll get used to it."

With a harsh look at his father, Roscoe turned away. . . .

X

At the termination of this interview, Benjamin wandered dismally upstairs and stared at himself in the mirror. He had not shaved for three months, but he could find nothing on his face but a faint white down with which it seemed unnecessary to meddle. When he had first come home from Harvard, Roscoe had approached him with the proposition that he should wear eye-glasses and imitation whiskers glued to his cheeks, and it had seemed for a moment that the farce of his early years was to be repeated. But whiskers had itched and made him ashamed. He wept and Roscoe had reluctantly relented.

Benjamin opened a book of boys' stories, "The Boy Scouts in Bimini Bay," and began to read. But he found himself thinking persistently about the war. America had joined the Allied cause during the preceding month, and Benjamin wanted to enlist, but, alas, sixteen was the minimum age, and he did not look that old. His true age, which was fifty-seven, would have disqualified him, anyway.

There was a knock at his door, and the butler appeared with a letter bearing a large official legend in the corner and addressed to Mr. Benjamin Button. Benjamin tore it open eagerly, and read the enclosure with delight. It informed him that many reserve officers who had served in the Spanish-American War were being called back into service with a higher rank, and it enclosed his commission as brigadier-general in the United States Army with orders to report immediately.

Benjamin jumped to his feet fairly quivering with enthusiasm. This was what he had wanted. He seized his cap and ten minutes later he had entered a large tailoring establishment on Charles Street, and asked in his uncertain treble to be measured for a uniform.

"Want to play soldier, sonny?" demanded a clerk, casually.

Benjamin flushed. "Say! Never mind what I want!" he retorted angrily. "My name's Button and I live on Mt. Vernon Place, so you know I'm good for it."

"Well," admitted the clerk, hesitantly, "if you're not, I guess your daddy is, all right."

Benjamin was measured, and a week later his uniform was completed. He had difficulty in obtaining the proper general's insignia because the dealer kept insisting to Benjamin that a nice Y.W.C.A. badge would look just as well and be much more fun to play with.

Saying nothing to Roscoe, he left the house one night and proceeded by train to Camp Mosby, in South Carolina, where he was to command an infantry brigade. On a sultry April day he approached the entrance to the camp, paid off the taxicab which had brought him from the station, and turned to the sentry on guard.

"Get someone to handle my luggage!" he said briskly.

The sentry eyed him reproachfully. "Say," he remarked, "where you goin' with the general's duds, sonny?"

Benjamin, veteran of the Spanish-American War, whirled upon him with fire in his eye, but with, alas, a changing treble voice.

"Come to attention!" he tried to thunder; he paused for breath — then suddenly he saw the sentry snap his heels together and bring his rifle to the present. Benjamin concealed a smile of gratification, but when he glanced around his smile faded. It was not he who had inspired obedience, but an imposing artillery colonel who was approaching on horseback.

"Colonel!" called Benjamin shrilly.

The colonel came up, drew rein, and looked coolly down at him

27

with a twinkle in his eyes. "Whose little boy are you?" he demanded kindly.

"I'll soon darn well show you whose little boy I am!" retorted Benjamin in a ferocious voice. "Get down off that horse!"

The colonel roared with laughter.

"You want him, eh, general?"

"Here!" cried Benjamin desperately. "Read this." And he thrust his commission toward the colonel.

The colonel read it, his eyes popping from their sockets.

"Where'd you get this?" he demanded, slipping the document into his own pocket.

"I got it from the Government, as you'll soon find out!"

"You come along with me," said the colonel with a peculiar look. "We'll go up to headquarters and talk this over. Come along."

The colonel turned and began walking his horse in the direction of headquarters. There was nothing for Benjamin to do but follow with as much dignity as possible—meanwhile promising himself a stern revenge.

But this revenge did not materialize. Two days later, however, his son Roscoe materialized from Baltimore, hot and cross from a hasty trip, and escorted the weeping general, *sans* uniform, back to his home.

XI

In 1920 Roscoe Button's first child was born. During the attendant festivities, however, no one thought it "the thing" to mention that the little grubby boy, apparently about ten years of age who played around the house with lead soldiers and a miniature circus, was the new baby's own grandfather.

No one disliked the little boy whose fresh, cheerful face was crossed with just a hint of sadness, but to Roscoe Button his presence was a source of torment. In the idiom of his generation Roscoe did not consider the matter "efficient." It seemed to him that his father, in refusing to look sixty, had not behaved like a "red-blooded he-man"—this was Roscoe's favorite expression—but in a curious and perverse manner. Indeed, to think about the matter for as much as a half an hour drove him to the edge of insanity. Roscoe believed that "live wires" should keep young, but carrying it out on such a scale was—was—was inefficient. And there Roscoe rested.

Five years later Roscoe's little boy had grown old enough to play childish games with little Benjamin under the supervision of the same nurse. Roscoe took them both to kindergarten on the same day and Benjamin found that playing with little strips of colored paper, making mats and chains and curious and beautiful designs, was the most fascinating game in the world. Once he was bad and had to stand in the corner—then he cried—but for the most part there were gay hours in the cheerful room, with the sunlight coming in the windows and Miss Bailey's kind hand resting for a moment now and then in his tousled hair.

Roscoe's son moved up into the first grade after a year, but Benjamin stayed on in the kindergarten. He was very happy. Sometimes when other tots talked about what they would do when they grew up a shadow would cross his little face as if in a dim, childish way he realized that those were things in which he was never to share.

The days flowed on in monotonous content. He went back a third year to the kindergarten, but he was too little now to understand what the bright shining strips of paper were for. He cried because the other boys were bigger than he and he was afraid of them. The teacher talked to him, but though he tried to understand he could not understand at all.

He was taken from the kindergarten. His nurse, Nana, in her starched gingham dress, became the center of his tiny world. On bright days they walked in the park; Nana would point at a great gray monster and say "elephant," and Benjamin would say it after her, and when he was being undressed for bed that night he would say it over and over aloud to her: "Elyphant, elyphant, elyphant." Sometimes Nana let him jump on the bed, which was fun, because if you sat down exactly right it would bounce you up on your feet again, and if you said "Ah" for a long time while you jumped you got a very pleasing broken vocal effect.

He loved to take a big cane from the hatrack and go around hitting chairs and tables with it and saying: "Fight, fight, fight." When there were people there the old ladies would cluck at him, which interested him, and the young ladies would try to kiss him, which he submitted to with mild boredom. And when the long day was done at five o'clock he would go upstairs with Nana and be fed oatmeal and nice soft mushy foods with a spoon.

There were no troublesome memories in his childish sleep; no token came to him of his brave days at college, of the glittering years when he flustered the hearts of many girls. There were only the white, safe walls of his crib and Nana and a man who came to see him sometimes, and a great big orange ball that Nana pointed at just before his twilight bed hour and called "sun." When the sun went his eyes were sleepy—there were no dreams, no dreams to haunt him.

The past—the wild charge at the head of his men up San Juan Hill; the first years of his marriage when he worked late into the summer dusk down in the busy city for young Hildegarde whom he loved; the days before that when he sat smoking far into the night in the gloomy old Button house on Monroe Street with his grandfather—all these had faded like unsubstantial dreams from his mind as though they had never been.

He did not remember. He did not remember clearly whether the milk was warm or cool at his last feeding or how the days passed—there was only his crib and Nana's familiar presence. And then he remembered nothing. When he was hungry he cried—that was all. Through the noons and nights he breathed and over him there were soft mumblings and murmurings that he scarcely heard, and faintly differentiated smells, and light and darkness.

Then it was all dark, and his white crib and the dim faces that moved above him, and the warm sweet aroma of the milk, faded out altogether from his mind.

The Curious Case Of
BENJAMIN BUTTON

SCREENPLAY BY

Eric Roth

SCREEN STORY BY

Eric Roth

AND

Robin Swicord

"The Curious Case of Benjamin Button"

As all things do, it begins in the dark. EYES blink
open. Blue eyes. The first thing they see is a WOMAN
near 40, sitting, looking out a window, watching the wind
blowing, rattling a window.

> A WOMAN'S (V.O.)
> What are you looking at Caroline?

> CAROLINE
> The wind, Ma... They say the
> hurricane is coming.

1   INT. HOSPITAL ROOM, NEW ORLEANS - MORNING, PRESENT   1

Now we see we're in a hospital room with layers of white
enamel paint trying without success to hide the years...
An old WOMAN, past 80, withered, still regal with a green
turban around her bald head is propped by pillows, her
blue eyes looking out at us from her bed... She's
connected to an intravenous for sustenance and a morphine
drip... Her name, is DAISY FULLER. She speaks with a
Southern lilt.

We see a young Black Woman, a "sitter," DOROTHY BAKER,
sitting by the bed, reading a newspaper, with one eye at
the window...

> DAISY
> I feel like I'm on a boat,
> drifting...

Caroline moves to take Dorothy's place.

> CAROLINE
> (tenderly)
> Can I do anything for you, Ma?
> Make anything easier?

> DAISY
> Oh, sugar, there's nothing left to
> do... It is what it is.
> I'm finding it harder to keep my
> eyes open...
> (and moving around)
> My mouth full of cotton...

(CONTINUED)

Agitated, she scratches at her nightgown as if it were
sticking to her... The Sitter gets up and straightens it for
her.

                    DOROTHY BAKER
          There, there, Miss Daisy... you'll
          scratch yourself to ribbons...

                    CAROLINE
          Do you want some more medication,
          Mother? The doctor said you can
          have as much as you want.

                    DOROTHY BAKER
          No need for anybody to suffer.

Daisy is quiet, looking into the distance... Caroline,
seeking closure, sits on the bed with her and takes her
hand.

                    CAROLINE
          A friend told me she never had the
          chance to say goodbye to her
          mother.

                    DAISY
          It's okay.

                    CAROLINE
          I wanted to ...I wanted to tell
          you how much I'm gonna miss you.

Caroline starts to cry and hugs Daisy. They hold each
other for some time.

                    DAISY
          Oh, Caroline.

                    CAROLINE
          Are you afraid?

                    DAISY
          I'm curious what comes next.

She closes her eyes... drifting with the morphine... and
a thought, a dream, a sound, crosses her mind...

                                              (CONTINUED)

Daisy looks off, a distant memory...

                    DAISY (CONT'D)
              They built the train station in
              1918. Your father was there the
              day it opened... He said they had
              a tuba band playing...

2   EXT. THE NEW TRAIN STATION, NEW ORLEANS - DAY, 1918   2

     And we see a TUBA BAND is playing while a ribbon cutting
     ceremony is taking place across the steps of the new
     TRAIN STATION...

                    DAISY
              They had the finest clockmaker in
              all of the south to build that
              glorious clock...

3   INT. CLOCKMAKER'S SHOP, NEW ORLEANS - NIGHT, 1917   3

     We see an old French Quarter storefront with an endless
     array of clocks and watches...

4   INT. THE HOSPITAL ROOM, NEW ORLEANS - MORNING, PRESENT   4

     The slightest of smiles crosses Daisy's lips... saying to
     herself again... "Mr. Cake..."

                    DAISY'S (V.O.)
              His name was Mr. Gateau, "Mr.
              Cake."

5   INT. CLOCKMAKER'S SHOP, NEW ORLEANS - MORNING, PRESENT   5

     We see a diminutive man in a frock coat with small,
     delicate hands, "Mr. Cake," working in his downstairs
     workshop. More than a few clocks strike midnight, a
     handsome Creole Woman comes into the workshop...

                    DAISY'S (V.O.)
              He was married to a Creole of
              Evangeline Parish and they had a
              son.

     Taking his arm, she helps him up to show him to his bed.

                                              (CONTINUED)

CONTINUED:

> DAISY'S (V.O.) (CONT'D)
> Mr. Gateau was from birth,
> absolutely blind.

6   INT. CLOCKMAKER'S SHOP, NEW ORLEANS - NIGHT, 1917   6

...The clockmaker, his fine hands blindly working...

> DAISY'S (V.O.)
> When their son was old enough he
> joined the army. They prayed God
> would keep him out of harm's way.

7   EXT. OLD TRAIN STATION, NEW ORLEANS - DAY, 1917   7

An old wooden barn of a building. Their son, hugging his
parents, getting on a flatbed train crowded with other
soldiers, pulling away... Mr. Gateau, blindly waving his
hat goodbye to his son...

> DAISY'S (V.O.)
> For months he did nothing but work
> on that clock.

8   INT. WORKSHOP BELOW THE CLOCKMAKER'S HOME - NIGHT, 1918   8

The sound of clocks' constant ticking. Mr. Gateau at
work...

> DAISY'S (V.O.)
> One day a letter came...

Blanche ... a letter in her hand...reads to her blind
husband...

> DAISY (V.O.)
> ...and Mr. Gateau, done for the
> night, went up alone to bed.

Mr. Gateau, blindly feeling his way up the stairs...

> DAISY'S (V.O.)
> And their son came home.

9   EXT. OLD TRAIN STATION, NEW ORLEANS - DAY, 1918   9

We see "Mr. Cake" in his familiar hat, his wife holding
his arm, standing among the rows of coffins.

                                             (CONTINUED)

> DAISY'S (V.O.)
> They buried him in the Gateau
> family plot where he would be with
> them when their time came.

10   EXT. NEW ORLEANS CEMETERY - DAY, 1918   10

An old New Orleans cemetery, vines crawling the
sepulchers.

> DAISY'S (V.O.)
> Mr. Cake returned to his clock...
> laboring to finish...

11   INT. THE CLOCK WORKSHOP, NEW ORLEANS - LATE NIGHT, 1918   11

Mr. Gateau blindly setting the last spring, closing up
the clock back... finished at last.

> DAISY'S (V.O.)
> It was a morning to remember...
> Papa said there were people
> everywhere...

12   INT. THE NEW TRAIN STATION, NEW ORLEANS - DAY, 1918   12

And we see a large throng gathered to watch the unveiling
of the clock. Politicians, citizens, and pickpockets
alike...

> DAISY'S (V.O.)
> Even Teddy Roosevelt came.

And we see the distinctive figure of Theodore Roosevelt,
in overcoat and hat, the war heavy on his shoulders. We
watch Mr. Cake, with the aid of an assistant, climbing
the scaffolding to his clock covered by a velvet drape...
He stands for a moment... and with a simple tug, releases
the purple swath... People gasp at the magnificent
clock... "Mr. Cake" winds the clock, which chimes a
glorious chime... Pushed by an angel, the second-hand
begins its eternal journey...going around... Everyone
cheers... until they realize the clock is going the wrong
way... traveling backwards in time... A man shouts, "It's
running backwards!"

(CONTINUED)

                              MONSIEUR GATEAU
                    I made it that way... so that
                    perhaps the boys that we lost in
                    the war might stand and come home
                    again...

13   EXT. BATTLEFIELD - DAY, 1918   13

        And we see just that... bullets leaving mens' wounds
        sailing back into the rifles from whence they came...
        limbs, whole again... cannon balls rocketing backwards
        into the cannons' breech... Fallen come to their feet, to
        live and breathe again.

                              MONSIEUR GATEAU (V.O.)
                    ... home to farm, to work, have
                    children, to live long, full
                    lives...

14   INT. THE NEW TRAIN STATION, NEW ORLEANS - DAY, 1918   14

        Teddy Roosevelt, bereft, removes his hat...

                              MONSIEUR GATEAU
                    Perhaps, my own son might come
                    home again...

15   EXT. OLD TRAIN STATION, NEW ORLEANS - DAY, ANOTHER TIME   15

        And we see his own son, Martin, once again full of life
        hopping backward off the train to land where his journey
        started... back in the arms of his loving parents...

16   INT. TRAIN STATION, NEW ORLEANS - DAY, 1918   16

                              MONSIEUR GATEAU
                    I'm sorry if I offended anybody. I
                    hope you enjoy my clock.

        Mr. Gateau makes his way down the steps of the
        platform.... The crowd is motionless. They look to Teddy
        Roosevelt for guidance... but he simply puts his hat on,
        and with his guardians, is gone...

> DAISY'S (V.O.)
> Mr. Cake was never seen again.
> Some say he died of a broken
> heart. Some said he went to
> sea...

17   EXT. THE MISSISSIPPI RIVER - AT THE END OF A DAY   17

Mr. Gateau, blindly rowing... away...

> DAISY'S (V.O.)
> He just rowed and rowed away...

18   INT. HOSPITAL ROOM, NEW ORLEANS - MORNING, PRESENT   18

The wind loudly rattles the window... they turn to
look...

> DOROTHY BAKER
> Excuse me, do you mind if I make a
> call? Somebody's watching my
> little boy.

> CAROLINE
> Sure.

It's quiet, Caroline sitting on the bed with her dying
mother... with the wind knocking at the window... After
some moments:

> CAROLINE (CONT'D)
> I hope I haven't disappointed you.

> DAISY
> You couldn't disappoint me.

> CAROLINE
> Well, I know I don't have much to
> show for myself...

> DAISY
> (importantly)
> Darlin' could you? In my dark
> suitcase. There's a diary.

Caroline doing what she's asked goes over to one of the
suitcases by the bed... She opens it...

(CONTINUED)

and among the clothes and the keepsakes, there is indeed
a brown leather diary.

> CAROLINE
> This?

> DAISY
> Could you read it to me?

> CAROLINE
> Is this what you want to do?

> DAISY
> I tried to read it a hundred
> different times...

Daisy closes her eyes... Caroline hesitates, she takes
out a sheaf of papers... It's a journal of some kind
written in longhand... Pages have come undone... scraps
of paper, even some napkins...

> CAROLINE
> Mom, it's not exactly...

> DAISY
>   (murmurs)
> It's just the sound of your voice
> darlin'...

> CAROLINE
> Okay.

And for her dying mother's sake she begins to read it:

> CAROLINE (CONT'D)
> It's dated "April 4, 1985." It
> says, "New Orleans."
>   (after a beat)
> "This is my last will and
> testament... I don't have much to
> leave... few possessions, no money
> really... I will go out of this
> world the same way I came in,
> alone, and with nothing. All I
> have is my story... I'm writing it
> now while I still remember it..."

(CONTINUED)

She looks over at her mother. But her mother's eyes are
closed... peaceful...

                    CAROLINE (CONT'D)
          "My name is Benjamin..."

And Caroline's voice becomes a MAN'S voice...

                    A MAN'S (V.O.)
          "Benjamin Button... and I was born
          under unusual circumstances."

19   EXT. NEW ORLEANS - NIGHT 1918   **19**

THERE'S SUDDENLY AN EXPLOSION OF FIREWORKS.

                    BENJAMIN BUTTON'S (V.O.)
          The First World War had ended.

We see the streets of New Orleans are filled with
drunken, singing revelers... cars jamming the
cobblestones, people kissing, shouting joyful... Another
burst of fireworks.

                    BENJAMIN BUTTON'S (V.O.) (CONT'D)
          And I had been told it was an
          especially good night to be
          born...

And we see in the fireworks' light, a young MAN in his
early 30s, THOMAS BUTTON, running up to the gate of a
fashionable town home. He nearly collides with a PRIEST
who arrives there at the same time. Thomas runs past
him, up the steps...

20   INT. BUTTON HOUSE, NEW ORLEANS - NIGHT 1918   **20**

...He runs past a solemn Maid and up a long staircase...
barging into the MASTER BEDROOM...

21   INT. MASTER BEDROOM, BUTTON HOUSE - NIGHT 1918   **21**

... where we see a young Woman is lying on a bloody bed,
frantically being administered to by a DOCTOR with the
help of the small domestic staff... the PRIEST enters...

                                        (CONTINUED)

> THOMAS BUTTON
> (seeing him)
> What are you doing here?

> THE DOCTOR
> Thomas, I'm afraid she's going to
> die...

The maids, bringing bedsheets, futilely start to change
her bloody linens...

> THOMAS BUTTON
> That's enough...! All of you! Get
> away from her!

They move out of the way... and Thomas kneels beside his
wife... She's pale white, fear in her soft brown eyes...
He takes her hand...

> THOMAS BUTTON (CONT'D)
> I came as quickly as I could...the
> streets are filled with people...

As if to underscore it, fireworks go off...

> HIS YOUNG WIFE
> Thomas, promise me he has a place.

And she is interrupted by the sudden CRY OF A BABY. But
Thomas can't take his eyes from his dying wife...

He doesn't understand... She looks up at him... holds his
hand tight... then she slips away... The Doctor listening
for her pulse... He covers her... it's quiet... the
Priest's murmured incantations... the housemaids
crying...

> BENJAMIN BUTTON'S (V.O.)
> She gave her life for me... And
> for that I am forever grateful...

When we hear again the BABY CRYING... The BABY'S CRY is
not quite right... It is not an infant's cry for succor,
or a natural cry to exercise its new lungs... It's a
deep, haunting cry from some primal soul... They all
turn, and the room stills... listening as The BABY
continues its mournful WAIL. Only Thomas goes to
answer...

                                                (CONTINUED)

The Baby in a basket, swaddled in a thick blanket, its
face covered with cloth... Thomas goes to lift it, to see
his son's face...

                    MAID
          Mr. Button...!

He lifts the cloth anyway... He recoils... for he has
seen some kind of horror... He makes the smallest of
sounds, a whispered "Ohhhh." And then he suddenly
snatches up the swaddled baby — running with it out of
the room... downstairs... outside...the Doctor calls
after him...

                    DOCTOR
          Thomas..Thomas..Where are you
          going?

22   EXT. NEW ORLEANS - NIGHT, 1918   **22**

... Thomas, tears on his face, carrying his CRYING BABY,
through the streets... Pushing through crowds...

23   EXT. A BRIDGE, NEW ORLEANS - NIGHT, 1918   **23**

... he comes along an old bridge over a waterway... the
air heavy with the haze of fireworks... the water dark...
brokenhearted, he lifts the baby to throw it into the
black water... He is just at the apex of this throw when,
despite his sadness, he can't bring himself to do it...
Instead, cradles the newborn...

                    THOMAS
          I'm sorry... I'm so sorry...

A LANTERN lights his face... A POLICEMAN down the way...

                    POLICEMAN
          What are you doing there!?

The BABY starts to CRY...

                    POLICEMAN (CONT'D)
          What do you have there?

Thomas takes off... the Policeman after him... Thomas,
carrying the CRYING BABY, running...

EXT. NEW ORLEANS, GARDEN DISTRICT - NIGHT, 1918

Thomas, scuttling with the crying infant through narrow
streets past the back porches and the back stairs of the
large old moldering antebellum houses...

EXT. THE BACK OF AN OLD NEW ORLEANS HOUSE - NIGHT, 1918

He comes to an old three-story house with a screened
porch. He ducks in the gate and the policeman runs past.
VOICES from inside... PEOPLE TALKING and LAUGHING... The
Baby, soothed by the soft yellow light, by the music of
the voices, by the house itself -- stops its mournful
cry. Thomas stops, catching his breath... the sounds of
VOICES coming... Thomas quietly sets the baby on the back
porch steps. He takes out every last dollar he has,
tucking the money inside the Baby's blanket... Suddenly
the screen door opens and Thomas backs around the corner.

When a young Black Woman, in a brown dress, comes onto
the porch... A thin, attractive woman, in her late 20s,
with the sultry eyes of a lounge singer -- She's known as
QUEENIE. She's followed by a handsome Black man, MR.
WEATHERS -- that everyone calls TIZZY.

She stands for a moment taking in the night air...

                    QUEENIE
          The air is sweet...

                    TIZZY
          You look very handsome tonight,
          Miss Queenie, handsome as I ever
          seen you... The brown matches
          your eyes...

Thomas, his decision made, turns, moving away from the
house, leaving his child behind.

                    QUEENIE
          Oh hush.
               (She swipes at him
               with her apron)
          You ain't no slouch yourself.

He smiles, tips his hat... And they stand in the quiet...

                                        (CONTINUED)

                       TIZZY
          Hambert's back in town... came
          home legless, but he home...
              (beat)
          I know you was sweet on him one
          time...

                    QUEENIE
          Sweeter than I shoulda been...

And as if right on cue an older white Woman sticks her
head out...

                  OLD WOMAN
          Ms. Simone messed herself...

                    QUEENIE
          Sweet Jesus, she's got to stop
          doing that, or it's diapers for
          her... I'll be right there,

The woman disappears inside. Queenie, not anxious to
go...Mr. Weathers grabs her hand and starts down the
stairs.

                    TIZZY
          Come on, it's awful nice out here
          ... Come on out back for a
          moment... take your mind off
          things...

He backs down the stairs, holding her hand, and he
suddenly steps right on top of the Baby... The baby
wails, Tizzy stumbles, nearly falls...

                TIZZY (CONT'D)
          What in God's name...?!!

She moves to it... pushes aside the blanket, and freezes.

It is the very first time we have seen the baby. What we
see is the prominent bald head of any newborn... but it
has the face, the wrinkled skin, the faded eyes, of an
octogenarian. Indeed, if we didn't know any better, it
would seem the newborn was a wrinkled decrepit sad-eyed
old man...

                            (CONTINUED)

                         QUEENIE
                Oh the Lord did something here...!

And they're both motionless, not quite sure what to do...

                         TIZZY
                I hope I didn't hurt it none...
                steppin' on it like that...

The BABY won't stop its mournful cry...

                         TIZZY (CONT'D)
                We best leave it to the police...
                I'll go --

Queenie hesitates... a longing.

                         QUEENIE
                It's for sure nobody wanted to
                keep it...C'mon, baby.

And making up her mind, she suddenly grabs up the crying
baby, taking it inside... Tizzy, anxiously whispering
something, going in after her...

25   INT. THE NOLAN HOUSE, NEW ORLEANS - NIGHT, 1918   25

A piano's playing a standard, people singing.... There's
a myriad of old dark rooms... heavy furniture and
carpets... an eclectic mixture of the possessions of
those who have lived and died here over many years... and
we see a parlor is crowded with Old People, from sixty to
ninety-five, in various stages of health... various
contraptions to keep them "afloat". An Old Age Home. We
see Queenie moving quietly along a hallway, carrying the
crying baby so as not to be seen. Tizzy, following her,
still anxiously whispering after her...

                         A WOMAN'S (V.O.)
                Where are you, Queenie...?

                         QUEENIE
                Hold your water...
                     (and to Tizzy)
                Go see to them.

He does what she asks. She hurries the baby into a small
room, literally like a mouse house, under the stairs...

INT. QUEENIE'S ROOM, OLD HOUSE, NEW ORLEANS - NIGHT 1918

A small room tucked under the staircase...

> A WOMAN'S (V.O.)
> Queenie Apple... she went and
> messed herself all over again...

> QUEENIE
> Jane Childress start her a bath...
> and mind your business, Mrs.
> Duprey... You'll be messing
> yourself soon enough!

There's a KNOCK on Queenie's door.

> A WOMAN'S (V.O.)
> (whispers)
> Somebody stole my necklace...

> QUEENIE
> Alright Mrs. Hollister, I'll be
> right with you...Go on back
> upstairs, you hear.

She whispers to The Baby, soothing it. And looking for a
place to put it, she opens a dresser drawer...

> QUEENIE (CONT'D)
> You are as ugly as an old pot...
> but you still a child of God...

> A WOMAN'S (V.O.)
> Queenie, Apple... she won't go
> take a bath wit'out you...

> QUEENIE
> Mercy, I'll be right there.

And with that she puts The Baby into the top dresser
drawer... with her unmentionables...

> QUEENIE (CONT'D)
> You just wait right here for me
> okay.

(CONTINUED)

She shuts it... leaving it open just a crack, enough to
breathe...she opens the door and there's an Old Woman,
looking very lost, looking in the room...

>   MRS. HOLLISTER
>   My sister gave those pearls to
>   me... I can't find them
>   anywhere... Somebody's been
>   stealing my jewelry...!

>   QUEENIE
>   They're right here, Mrs.
>   Hollister, see, right 'round your
>   pretty white neck...
>   (moving her)
>   Come on now...hush all that noise.
>   Is Dr. Rose still here?

Queenie takes a concerned look back at the Baby, and
closes the door... And we stay behind for a moment...
inside Queenie's underwear drawer, with the smell of a
lilac sachet... is the Baby with the face of an old
man... looking up at the sliver of light coming into the
dresser drawer...

27   INT. PARLOR, NOLAN HOUSE, NEW ORLEANS - NIGHT, 1918   27

We see the Doctor, an older man in a tired suit, who has
done this longer than he cares to remember, finishing
examining one of the elderly boarders.

>   DR. ROSE
>   Your heart is strong. Try to avoid
>   any undue stimulation. I trust you
>   ladies will help me out with that.

The boarders laugh. Queenie comes beside him, saying
something...

28   INT. QUEENIE'S ROOM - THAT NIGHT, 1918   28

The Baby is lying on Queenie's bed... Dr. Rose,
stethoscope ever dangling, washes his hands in a sink.

>   DOCTOR ROSE
>   ... He's nearly blind from
>   cataracts...
>   (MORE)

                                              (CONTINUED)

                    DOCTOR ROSE (CONT'D)
          I'm not sure if he can hear... His
          bones indicate severe arthritis...
          His skin has lost all
          elasticity... His hands and feet
          are ossified... He has all the
          deterioration, the infirmities,
          not of a newborn, but of a man
          well in his eighties on the way to
          his grave...

                    QUEENIE
          You mean to say he's dying?

                    DOCTOR ROSE
          His body is failing him before his
          life's begun.

They're still, looking at the strange baby.

                    DOCTOR ROSE (CONT'D)
          Where did he come from?

                    QUEENIE
             (after a beat)
          It's my sister's child... From
          Lafayette. She had an unfortunate
          adventure.
             (whispers)
          The poor child got the worse of
          it... come out white...

                    DOCTOR ROSE
          There are places for 'unwanted'
          babies like these, Queenie...
          There's no room for another mouth
          to feed here... The Nolan
          Foundation, despite their good
          intentions, thinks this place is a
          large nuisance as it is... A baby
          here --

                    QUEENIE
             (appealing)
          You said he don't have long.

                    DOCTOR ROSE
          Queenie -- some creatures aren't
          meant to survive.

                                        (CONTINUED)

She looks at the Baby, determined.

                    QUEENIE
          No, this baby, he is a miracle,
          that's for certain... just not the
          kind of miracle one hopes to
          see...

29   INT. PARLOR, NOLAN HOUSE - THAT NIGHT, 1918   29

The Old People are sitting around the parlor talking,
playing cards... Queenie brings the baby bundle into the
room.

                    QUEENIE
          You all listen...

And they stop what they are doing...

                    QUEENIE (CONT'D)
          We gonna have us a visitor that
          will be staying with us for a
          little while... My sister had a
          child but couldn't see right by
          it... He's known as...
               (a hesitation naming him)
          Benjamin...
               (she likes the sound
                of it)
          Benjamin... He's not a well
          child... so we gonna have to take
          good care of him...

We see Tizzy's come out of the kitchen, watching with an
air of strong disapproval... And an OLD WOMAN says...

                    ONE OF THE WOMEN
          I had ten children... there's not
          a baby I can't care for... let me
          see him...

Queenie hesitates, and shows the Baby to her... The Old
Woman looks at the baby's face...

                                              (CONTINUED)

> THE OLD WOMAN
> (startled)
> God in heaven, he looks just like
> my ex-husband...

And there's laughter...

> QUEENIE
> He's prematurely old... Doctor
> Rose said he don't have much more
> time on this earth...

> A MAN
> Join the club.

They all laugh. Their laughter makes the baby seem to
smile... the lonely smile of an old, dying man.

30   INT. QUEENIE'S ROOM - STILL LATER THAT NIGHT, 1918   30

We see Queenie, unable to sleep, lying in bed, looking
down at the baby...there's a light KNOCK on the door...
Tizzy...

> TIZZY
> Hambert sends his remembrances to
> you.

She nods... The baby cries out... and then it's
quiet...Tizzy moves to sit on the bed and looks down at
the baby.

> TIZZY (CONT'D)
> (meaning the baby)
> Are you right out of your mind? I
> know you don't got all the parts
> it takes to make one of your
> own... but this isn't yours to
> keep... it may not even be human
> kind...

With nothing left to be said, he starts to go...

> QUEENIE
> (whispers)
> Mr. Weathers come back here!
> Please.

(CONTINUED)

He slows. She's quiet. And she whispers:

> QUEENIE (CONT'D)
> "You never know what's comin' for
> you."

And as they move to be with one another, to make love; we
look over at the dresser drawer... Benjamin lying among
the unmentionables, looking out at the world...

> BENJAMIN BUTTON'S (V.O.)
> It seemed I'd found a home...

31   INT. THE HOSPITAL ROOM, NEW ORLEANS - DAY, PRESENT   31

Caroline with the journal on her knees. Daisy, eyes
closed... the wind gathered in strength... furiously
knocking...

> CAROLINE
> Is any of this true?

> DAISY
> You have such a lovely voice.

She looks through the book...She discovers inside...

> CAROLINE
> Mom, an ancient streetcar token.

She gives it to her mother, folding her hand around it.
But Daisy is somewhere else, looking out the window...

> DAISY
> That clock just kept going, year
> after year after year...

32   INT. "NEW" TRAIN STATION, NEW ORLEANS - ANOTHER DAY, 1925   32

And we see "Mr. Cake's" clock with its cherubs pushing
the "hands of progress," still marking time backwards...
The year is now, "1925..."

INT. THE NOLAN HOUSE - DINING ROOM, NEW ORLEANS -
EVENING, 1925

                         BENJAMIN BUTTON'S (V.O.)
          ...I didn't know I was a child. I
          thought I was like everyone else
          who lived there, an old man, in
          the "twilight" of his life.

The boarders eating dinner. Queenie, in a white
uniform... along with Tizzy, wearing a chef's hat and
apron, helping her serve. We move across the ancient
faces... until we come to one particular face... Wearing
eyeglasses now... but the same wrinkled face we've come
to know... the face of a very old man... The face of
Benjamin Button, when he should normally be a six-year-
old. He's sitting in a wheelchair now... small,
shrunken, hunched with age, legs and hands crippled with
arthritis... Eyeglasses are just one addition... a
hearing aid... a bulky apparatus of its time, is in one
ear... But if we look even closer we can see there are
sprouts of hair... wisps of white... what would be the
last hair for some... seem to be growing in... As we
watch him eat, he uses his fork like a child might,
banging it just for the hell of it making noise...

                         QUEENIE
          Stop bangin' that fork...
                (fixing it in his
                 arthritic hand)
          It's for eating, not for playin'
          with... And use your napkin,
          please Mr. Benjamin...

And he does as he's told... A staff member helps one of
the old men, feeding him... Benjamin just another old man
having dinner with his contemporaries.

EXT. THE PORCH, NOLAN HOUSE, NEW ORLEANS - NIGHT, 1925

A line of old people in rockers. Benjamin, like any six-
year-old, bored, wheels his chair back and forth, between
them... until one of the oldsters, who has had enough,
sticks his cane in the spokes of his wheelchair, making
him come to an abrupt stop... Sounds drift from the
street beyond the gate... children playing... people
talking...

                                        (CONTINUED)

                              BENJAMIN BUTTON'S (V.O.)
                         I always had a healthy curiosity.
                         What was up the street? Or around
                         the next corner?

Nobody says anything, rocking. Benjamin, eternally
curious needing to know, suddenly wheels himself
precariously to the very edge of the porch where he just
sees the street... children running on the street,
playing... carriages dropping people off for a party...
He leans forward to get an even better view... When
Queenie suddenly grabs him...

                         QUEENIE
                         Benjamin! That's dangerous... Come
                         back over here...! Stay put child!

...Rolling his wheelchair away from the edge to the
safety of the old people... out of sight of the street...

35   INT. QUEENIE'S ROOM - NIGHT, 1925   35

The small room with the small window. We see Benjamin in
a bed made on the floor... Queenie in her bed...

                         BENJAMIN BUTTON'S (V.O.)
                         I loved her very much. She was my
                         mother.

And he reaches to hold her hand. She generously takes
his hand... And they lay like that holding hands, Queenie
in bed, her "son", the "old man" on the floor...

                         BENJAMIN BUTTON
                         Momma...Momma... Some days I feel
                         different than the day before...

                         QUEENIE
                         Everybody feels different about
                         themselves one way or another. We
                         all goin' the same way, just
                         taking different roads to get
                         there that's all... You're on your
                         own road, Benjamin.

                         BENJAMIN BUTTON
                         Momma, how much longer do I got?

                                                  (CONTINUED)

> QUEENIE
> Just be thankful for what you're
> given, hear. You already here
> longer than you supposed to be.

We see the door quietly open, Tizzy coming in...

> BENJAMIN BUTTON'S (V.O.)
> Some nights, I'd have to sleep
> alone.

He looks at Benjamin, his signal to pick him up, carrying him out of the room, sitting him in his wheelchair, Tizzy going back down into the room to be with Queenie... shutting the door...

36   INT. THE PARLOR, NOLAN HOUSE, LATE AT NIGHT, 1925   **36**

An Old Woman's fallen fast asleep in an easy chair, a book on her lap. Benjamin sitting alone in his wheelchair, listening to the sounds of the house.

> BENJAMIN BUTTON'S (V.O.)
> I didn't mind. I would listen to
> the house breathing. All those
> people sleeping. I felt safe.

Be he still wants to know "What's over there?" He wheels himself over to sit at the door, looking outside... looking at the streetlights, the world beyond the gate... trying to see what's dangerous...

> BENJAMIN BUTTON'S (V.O.) (CONT'D)
> It was a place of great routine...
> Every morning at 5:30, no matter
> the weather... General Winslow,
> U.S. Army Retired... would raise
> the flag...

37   EXT. THE FRONT LAWN, NOLAN HOUSE - MORNING, 1925   **37**

And we see the very elderly General Winslow, doing just that... raising the flag in a downpour, only... he's naked. And as Queenie comes running across the lawn with a coat for him.

37A   OMITTED   37A

There's the sound of SOMEONE SINGING OPERA...

                    BENJAMIN BUTTON (V.O.)
               Mrs. Sybil Wagner, once an opera
               singer of some note... well, she'd
               sing Wagner...

38   INT. MRS. WAGNER'S ROOM, NOLAN HOUSE - MORNING, 1925   38

We see a Victrola playing, Mrs. Wagner at a window
singing with the musical accompaniment at the top of her
lungs... while, down the hall we see Queenie giving
Benjamin a bath... massaging his poor crippled legs...

                    QUEENIE
               C'mon baby, we're gonna put some
               life into these old sticks for
               you... get you walkin'...so you
               can help out around here.

39   OMITTED   39

                    BENJAMIN BUTTON'S (V.O.)
               No matter the season, supper was
               served promptly at 5:30.

40   INT. KITCHEN, NOLAN HOUSE - NIGHT, 1925   40

Tizzy washing dishes...Benjamin working with him...
reading from one of the labels on the cans...

                    BENJAMIN
               Mol--asses...

                    TIZZY
               "Molasses"...

                    BENJAMIN
               Molasses

And while washing the dishes...

                                                    .(CONTINUED)

                              TIZZY
                    I learned to read when I was five.
                    My grandfather was a dresser for a
                    famous actor. He'd brought every
                    play for me to read.
                         (Shakespeare)
                    "Kind keepers of my weak decaying
                    age, let dying Mortimer here rest
                    himself. Even like a man new
                    haled from the rack. So fare my
                    limbs with long imprisonment. And
                    these gray locks, the pursuivants
                    of death. Argue the end of Edmund
                    Mortimer."

Benjamin's mouth agape, awed, taken by him, his majesty.

                         TIZZY (CONT'D)
                    You thought I was plain ignorant,
                    didn't you?

Benjamin never thought about it...

                         TIZZY (CONT'D)
                    The actor my grandfather worked
                    for was John Wilkes Booth. He
                    killed Abraham Lincoln. You never
                    know what's coming for you.

                         BENJAMIN BUTTON'S (V.O.)
                    On Saturday nights Mama would make
                    me go to church...

41   INT. CHURCH TENT, NEW ORLEANS - A SATURDAY NIGHT, 1926   41

A sweltering shout 'em up Negro gospel tent. As they
listen to the choir Queenie looks over at Benjamin fast
asleep.

Queenie pushes Benjamin in his wheelchair past a line of
people looking to be healed, bringing him face to face
with a mountain of a PREACHER, pouring sweat and full of
fire...

                         THE PREACHER
                    What can I do for you, Sister?

                                                        (CONTINUED)

And Queenie whispers something to him.

                    THE PREACHER (CONT'D)
              Her parts are all twisted up
              inside so she can't have little
              children...

He puts his hand on her stomach...

                    PREACHER
              Lord, if you could see clear to
              forgive this woman her sins so she
              can bear the fruit of the womb.
                    (and shouts)
              Out damnable affliction!

He presses on her stomach... making Queenie nearly fall
over... held up by a "NURSE" in a crisp white uniform.
And once she's regained her balance...

                    THE PREACHER
              Praise God! Hallelujah!
                    (at Benjamin)
              And what's this old man's
              irrediction?

                    QUEENIE
              He's got the devil on his back...
              trying to ride him into the grave
              before his time...

                    THE PREACHER
                    (touches Benjamin)
              Out, Zebuchar! Out, Beelzebub!
                    (after a beat)
              How old are you?

And he says what is only true.

                    BENJAMIN
              I'm seven, but I look a lot older.

                    PREACHER
                    (laughs)
              God bless you. He's seven!

The congregation laughs...

                                        (CONTINUED)

> THE PREACHER
> This is a man who has optimism in
> his heart! Belief in his soul!
> We are all children in the eyes of
> God. Now we are going to get you
> out of that chair... we're gonna
> have you walk...
>> (his hands on Ben's
>> shoulders)
> In the name of God's glory, rise
> up!

And Benjamin, doing what he's asked, barely able to, his
legs akimbo, stands... The people all applaud...

> THE PREACHER (CONT'D)
> Now God is going to see you the
> rest of the way... He's going to
> see this little old man walk
> without the use of a crutch or a
> cane...! He's going to see that
> you walk by himself on faith and
> divine inspiration alone...! Now
> walk on...!

And Benjamin takes two very precarious steps and his poor
arthritic legs give out... and he sprawls to the floor...
Queenie and the Aides in white nurse's uniforms move to
help, but:

> THE PREACHER (CONT'D)
> Don't touch him!
>> (to Benjamin)
> Rise up, old man!

But Benjamin stays crumpled on the floor... The Preacher
comes to his feet, standing like a mountain over him...

> THE PREACHER (CONT'D)
> Rise up like Lazarus!

Benjamin still lies on the floor...

> THE PREACHER (CONT'D)
> I said rise up!!

And Benjamin, slowly but surely, makes his way to his
feet...

                    THE PREACHER (CONT'D)
          Yes. Come on, say hallelujah!
               (Hallelujah!)
          Now walk, my old friend...
          Walk on...!

And Benjamin, one crippled leg at a time, hobbles across
the stage... The people urging him on... a string of
"Hallelujahs...!" Queenie comes to join him... urging
him...

                    QUEENIE
          That's right Benjamin, that's
          right. Let the Lord carry you...

...The Preacher, walking along with him, more a dance
than a walk, shouting the name of the Lord... Queenie and
The Preacher walking Benjamin across the stage...
Benjamin making it to the other end... to a roar of
"Amens"!

                    BENJAMIN BUTTON'S (V.O.)
          Now, when I look back on it, it
          was kind of miraculous... But you
          know the saying, "...the Lord
          Giveth and the Lord Taketh
          away..."

... That mountain of a Preacher... in full exaltation to
God...

                    THE PREACHER
          Praise be to the Lord on the
          highest...!

Suddenly pitches over, flat on his face... Having had a
spontaneous coronary... lying center-stage, deader than
the proverbial doornail... The crisp uniformed "nurses"
running to attend to him, and poor "old" Benjamin
haplessly looking around.

42   INT. THE PARLOR ROOM, NOLAN HOUSE - ANOTHER DAY 1926   42

The people are gathered...

                                              (CONTINUED)

> BENJAMIN BUTTON'S (V.O.)
> There were so many birthdays...So
> we wouldn't run out, we would
> spare the candles.

A lit cake is being brought in celebrating General
Winslow's birthday. He stares at the cake, unhappily.

> GENERAL WINSLOW
> You know I don't like birthdays
> and I don't like cake.

He gets up, mutters something... and leaves. The
oldsters eye the cake, and without a moment's hesitation,
dig in...

> BENJAMIN BUTTON (V.O.)
> And death was a common visitor...
> People came and went...

43   EXT. NOLAN HOUSE, ANOTHER MORNING, 1926   43

Mrs. Wagner's window open... and not a sound coming
out...

> BENJAMIN BUTTON'S (V.O.)
> You always knew when someone left
> us... there was a silence in the
> house...

44   EXT. AN OLD NEW ORLEANS CEMETERY - DAY, 1926   44

A small funeral at an old cemetery... And while "DIE
VALKYRIE" PLAYS on her crank VICTROLA, an old man bangs
cymbals as a grand finale to the music... while we see
SYBIL WAGNER, laid to rest to sing in another choir:

45   EXT. THE BACK PORCH, THE NOLAN HOUSE - DUSK 1927   45

Benjamin with his wondrous ancient face sitting in his
wheelchair with the old people on the porch...watching
the sun go down...

> BENJAMIN BUTTON'S (V.O.)
> It was a wonderful place to grow
> up.
>   (MORE)

                                              (CONTINUED)

                          BENJAMIN BUTTON'S (V.O.) (CONT'D)
                    I was with people who had shed all
                    the inconsequences of earlier
                    life, left wondering about the
                    weather....the temperature of a
                    bath...the light at the end of the
                    day...

As one of them, as if to underscore the point, farts...

                          BENJAMIN BUTTON'S (V.O.)
                          (CONT'D)
                    For everyone that died, someone
                    would come to take their place.

46-47A OMITTED   **46-47A**

47B INT. THE NOLAN HOUSE, KITCHEN - ANOTHER DAY, 1927   **47B**

And we see Benjamin coming into the kitchen...Tizzy busy
preparing lunch...Benjamin stops, seeing a tiny African
man, his back to us, surrounded by old people sitting on
the lawn... He hears him telling them...

                    NGUNDA OTI
               I've been married five times....My
               first wife and I are captured by
               neighbor tribe of cannibals.

The old people shrink at the mention...

                    NGUNDA OTI (CONT'D)
               We escaped across the river...My
               wife, she can't swim, so sadly she
               eaten.

Tizzy comes in the door and sees Benjamin looking out the
window.

                    NGUNDA OTI (CONT'D)
               My second wife steps on cobra and
               dies...It was very bad luck to be
               married to me.

They laugh.

                    TIZZY
               That's Mr. Oti...He's an
               acquaintance of an acquaintance of
               mine...he's a pygmy.

                                              (CONTINUED)

>   NGUNDA OTI
>   The next summer I am captured
>   along with six others by the
>   Baschiele tribe. They trade us for
>   figs and shoes to a very strange
>   American man.

He instinctively turns and sees Benjamin standing in the
doorway watching him. When Mr. Oti spots him he quickly
ducks out of sight.

47C   OMITTED   **47C**

47D   INT. PARLOR, NOLAN HOUSE - ANOTHER TIME, 1927   **47D**

Benjamin is sitting on the sofa and Mr. Oti sits beside
him.

>   NGUNDA OTI
>   I hear you not so old as you
>   looking. You just foolin'
>   everybody. What's the matter? Did
>   you get Madjembe?

>   BENJAMIN
>   What's madjembe?

>   NGUNDA OTI
>   Worms.

>   BENJAMIN
>   I don't think I had worms. This is
>   just how I am.

Mr. Oti looks out at the street.

>   NGUNDA OTI
>   Come. Let's go get a cold root
>   beer?

>   BENJAMIN
>   (an echo)
>   I'm not supposed to. It's
>   dangerous.

>   NGUNDA OTI
>   Who said that?

                                                    (CONTINUED)

He gets up ready to go. Benjamin hesitates. He can see
Queenie busy going up the stairs.

> NGUNDA OTI (CONT'D)
> (last chance)
> ...Come on little man...

Despite knowing the consequences he takes up his canes
and follows Ngunda outside...

48   OMITTED   48

49   EXT. STREET, OUTSIDE NOLAN HOUSE, NEW ORLEANS - DAY, 1927   49

They come outside. Children on the street playing. Seeing
Benjamin, they come to a dead stop...staring at the freak
from the old people's home with another freak... Mr. Oti
suddenly runs into the street...

> NGUNDA OTI
> Hold please...

Benjamin tries as best he can to keep up... Mr. Oti darts
directly in front of a streetcar, shouting, making it
come to an abrupt stop...

50   INT. THE STREETCAR, NEW ORLEANS - DAY, 1927   50

Benjamin and Ngunda sitting in the seats behind a movable
metal bar that has "Coloreds" painted on it. A group of
school children nearby can't take their eyes off the two
of them.

> NGUNDA OTI
> Then I am in the monkey house at
> "Philadelphia Zoological Park."
> Three thousand people show up my
> first day...

He takes his wallet out, taking out a folded piece of
newspaper, shows it to Benjamin... "Bushman shares cage
with park apes."

> BENJAMIN
> What's it like living in a cage?

                                                    (CONTINUED)

> NGUNDA OTI
>
> It stinks. But the monkeys, they
> do some tricks... I throw a
> spear... I wrestle with Kowali,
> she is orangutan... When I'm not
> playing with monkeys -- they want
> me to run to bars in my cage with
> my teeth...

And he suddenly jumps up and does just that, charging
with his teeth bared, at the school children... They
scream... Mr. Oti, taking his seat again, laughs.
Benjamin laughs.

51   EXT. THE PERISTYLE, NEW ORLEANS - PARK - END OF DAY, 1927   **51**

Mr. Oti and Benjamin sit on a bench. Benjamin drinks a
soda and Mr. Oti takes a sip from his flask now and then.

> NGUNDA OTI
>
> Then I leave zoo. Go here. Go
> there. Wander most of the time.

> BENJAMIN
>
> You all alone?

> NGUNDA OTI
>
> Plenty times you be alone. When
> you different like us, it's gonna
> be that way. But I tell you a
> little secret. Fat people, skinny
> people, tall people, white
> people...they just as alone as we
> are...But they scared shitless.

He takes a healthy slug from flask...

> NGUNDA OTI (CONT'D)
>
> I think about the river I grew up
> on. It would be nice to sit by my
> river again.

He looks at his watch. He suddenly gets up...

> NGUNDA OTI (CONT'D)
>
> Come, I have an appointment.

EXT. BOURBON STREET CORNER, NEW ORLEANS - DUSK, 1927

Mr. Oti and Benjamin coming along the street, music pouring out... They reach a corner where a tall octoroon woman is waiting. She broadly smiles seeing Mr. Oti.

                    THE WOMAN
          There's my little man. You ready,
          sugar.

                    NGUNDA OTI
               (smiles, pure Ngunda)
          Always ready. Always ready.
               (introduces)
          Filamena, Mr. Benjamin.

                    FILAMENA GILEA
               (respectful of his
                age)
          It's a pleasure to meet you, Sir.

                    BENJAMIN BUTTON
          My pleasure ma'am.

                    NGUNDA OTI
               (to Benjamin)
          You can find your own way home,
          can't you?

Although he's not sure he can... he nods, yes.

                    NGUNDA OTI (CONT'D)
          Take the St. Charles line to
          Napoleon...

And with that, his arm around Filamena's waist, the two of them laughing, walk off... Benjamin's left standing on the street corner... he looks around to get his bearings... he moves along Bourbon Street... A streetcar comes along, bell clanging, it rushes by him... he yells to try to stop it...he watches it go... Clasping his canes, determined, he starts walking... bent over, one cane after the other... making his way along the street...as day turns to night...

EXT. NOLAN HOUSE, NEW ORLEANS - LATE NIGHT, 1927

We see Benjamin coming back to the gate... and we hear:
                                        (CONTINUED)

                          QUEENIE (V.O.)
                Where in God's name have you
                been?!! Get in here!

And we see Queenie opening the back window... She's
worried sick...

54   INT. KITCHEN, QUEENIE'S SINK, NOLAN HOUSE - NIGHT   54

Queenie cleaning his hands. They have been bleeding from
the blisters...

                          QUEENIE
                You take my breath away you know
                that...Oh Lord I was so worried
                about you...

Queenie leaves him.

                          BENJAMIN (V.O.)
                It had been the best day of my
                life.

55   INT. HOSPITAL ROOM, NEW ORLEANS - MORNING, PRESENT   55

And the "caregiver," Dorothy Baker, comes back in. She
feels Daisy's pulse, straightens her pillow...

                          DOROTHY BAKER
                How's her breathing...

                          CAROLINE
                It's shallow.

                          DOROTHY BAKER
                They say it'll reach us in a few
                hours... I got to get my baby and
                take him to my sister's... they
                say there's nothin' to worry about
                here in the hospital. Nurses are
                right here if you need them....Are
                you okay?

                          CAROLINE
                Yeah I'm okay reading but...

                                              (CONTINUED)

                              DOROTHY BAKER
                    ...It shouldn't be more than an
                    hour.

She leaves. It's momentarily quiet, the wind knocking at
the window... Daisy, ruminating not at all logical...

                              DAISY
                    Was that just company?

                              CAROLINE
                    Just Dorothy leaving.

                              DAISY
                    Go on Caroline.

Caroline looks. Daisy closes her eyes...

                              CAROLINE
                    "On Sundays the families would
                    come and visit...

56   EXT. THE LAWN, THE NOLAN HOUSE - DAY, 1930   56

The boarders on the lawn with their loved ones... And we
see an OLD MAN, walking with the aid of a cane come out
of the house onto the lawn... And as he comes closer we
see it's Benjamin. He's standing more upright now, a
distinctive shock of white hair, eyebrows, and beard...A
distinguished looking man in his seventies, or, in normal
years, a growing twelve-year-old boy...

                              BENJAMIN BUTTON'S (V.O.)
                    It was Thanksgiving 1930, I met
                    the person who changed my life
                    forever.

A chauffeured car has stopped... A man is standing in the
road, looking at the house through the gates... And we
realize it's THOMAS BUTTON... looking for a glimpse of
his son... Benjamin instinctively turns, but it's too
late, his father's back in the car, being driven away...

                              BENJAMIN BUTTON'S (V.O.) (CONT'D)
                    I noticed from time to time a car
                    stopped. A man who seemed to be
                    looking for someone.

                              (MORE)   (CONTINUED)

                          BENJAMIN BUTTON'S (V.O.) (CONT'D)

                    A WOMAN'S (V.O.)
              Well Benjamin, might I say you are
              looking strikingly youthful...

He turns, an older woman nearby...

                    BENJAMIN
                 (politely)
              Why, good day Mrs. Fuller...

                    GRANDMA FULLER
              A single cane, your back as
              straight as an arrow...what elixir
              have you been drinking?

                    BENJAMIN
              Thank you ma'am.

He laughs...And there's a voice that cuts through the
day...

                    A LITTLE GIRL'S VOICE
              Grandma, look at me...

Benjamin and Grandma Fuller turn to see a little girl, no
more than eight, doing pirouettes, one after another, for
an admiring group of old people...she full curtsies,
bowing -- the way dancers do head to chest...then raising
her head, laughing...

                    GRANDMA FULLER
              Now that was really something
              ...Come on over here, you...Now
              this is my granddaughter Daisy...
              This is Mr... I'm afraid,
              Benjamin, I don't rightly know
              your last name...

                    BENJAMIN
              Benjamin is just fine.

                    BENJAMIN BUTTON'S (V.O.)
              I never forgot her blue eyes.

                                        (CONTINUED)

                           TIZZY
                     (calling to all)
              Good people, supper is served...

57   INT. DINING ROOM, NOLAN HOUSE - THANKSGIVING, 1930   57

        The families, along with Ngunda and Filamena, are
        gathered in the dining room, their heads bowed in prayer.
        We see Daisy across from Benjamin...

                           MR. DAWS
                    ...for love and friends, for
                    everything thy goodness sends.
                    Amen.

        The prayer's finished, it's noisy...

                           DAISY
                     (looking at the food)
                    Did you know turkeys aren't really
                    birds...?

                           BENJAMIN
                    Why do you say that?

                           DAISY
                    They're in the pheasant family.
                    They can hardly fly. It's sad,
                    don't you think? A bird that
                    can't fly.

                           NGUNDA OTI
                    I like birds that can't fly. They
                    are so delicious.

                           DAISY
                    You're terrible.

                           QUEENIE
                     (standing)
                    I have something to tell you
                    all...

        They're quiet.

                           QUEENIE (CONT'D)
                    While we're giving thanks for
                    God's blessings...
                         (MORE)   (CONTINUED)

                              QUEENIE (CONT'D)
                    I've had a miracle happen.
                         (she touches her
                          stomach)
                    The Lord saw fit to answer my
                    prayers.

The people applaud the good news.

                              BENJAMIN
                    What does she mean "answered her
                    prayers?"

                              DAISY
                    She's going to have a baby, silly.
                    That's what my mother said when I
                    was going to have a baby brother
                    but he didn't live long because
                    he didn't breathe right...

And we can see Benjamin's heart beginning to break... he
looks over, Tizzy, proudly smiling... And as Queenie
accepts congratulations... Benjamin's old wrinkled face,
watching her... looks like he's going to cry...

58   INT. PARLOR, NOLAN HOUSE - NIGHT, LATER, 1930   **58**

We see an ABSTRACT BLACK AND WHITE DRAWING. And we hear
a Woman's voice...

                              A WOMAN'S (V.O.)
                    ...at five in the afternoon, when
                    he had got his beautiful hind legs
                    just as Big God Nqong had
                    promised. You can see that it is
                    five o'clock, because Big God
                    Nqong's pet tame clock says so.

AN OLD FINGER comes in pointing to a drawing. We see
Benjamin and Daisy, sitting close together on a sofa, and
Daisy's grandmother, arm encircling them, is reading to
them from Rudyard Kipling's "Just So Stories." Benjamin
and Daisy, sit rapt, when Grandmother Fuller finishes...

                              GRANDMA FULLER
                    Isn't that something?

Both Daisy and Benjamin, thrilled, say:

                                                        (CONTINUED)

                          DAISY
             Again. Read it again.

                          BENJAMIN
             Oh, read it again, please.

                          GRANDMA FULLER
             Alright, but afterwards you must
             go to bed.

                          DAISY
             I promise.

And that's just what she does... reading it again to
them... Benjamin and Daisy sitting shoulder to shoulder
in the crook of her arm...

59   INT. A ROOM, NOLAN HOUSE - LATE AT NIGHT, 1930   59

We see Benjamin asleep in bed with one of the Old Men,
MR. DAWS. The door opens. And Daisy, in her nightgown,
has come inside... she slightly touches Benjamin...

                          DAISY
                    (whispers)
             Are you sleeping?

                          BENJAMIN
                    (getting up)
             Who's that?

                          DAISY
             It's me, Daisy.

                          BENJAMIN
                    (puts on his glasses)
             Oh, hi.

                          DAISY
                    (whispers)
             Come on...

She moves quickly out of the room and Benjamin gets up,
and with the aid of his cane, follows her...

INT. BACK STAIRWELL, NOLAN HOUSE - LATE NIGHT, 1930

The old house still. Daisy, moving quietly down the
stairs. Benjamin, his cane softly thumping the steps,
following her.

> BENJAMIN
> (whispers)
> Where are we going?

She doesn't say anything. She leads him into the DINING
ROOM... where we see the wash has been draped, sheets and
pillowcases, like ghosts over the dining room table, and
a smaller side table, and a buffet...to dry...

> DAISY
> C'mon. Under here...

And she ducks under a sheet, beneath the dining table...
Benjamin follows her into the "fort..."

They sit... The little girl, and the old man with the
maturity of a ten year old boy, enjoying their secret
lair... She takes a candle out of the folds of her
nightgown... She tries to light it, but doesn't really
know how to use matches...

> DAISY (CONT'D)
> Here, you light it?

> BENJAMIN
> I'm not supposed to play with
> matches...

> DAISY
> Don't be chicken, light it...

Despite his caution, he lights the candle... the
candlelight making it feel more secret...

> DAISY (CONT'D)
> I'll tell you a secret if you tell
> me one...

> BENJAMIN
> Okay.

                                        (CONTINUED)

>   DAISY
>   (whispers)
>   I saw my momma kissing another
>   man. Her face was red from it.

Benjamin doesn't know what to say.

>   DAISY (CONT'D)
>   Your turn.

>   BENJAMIN
>   I'm not as old as I look.

>   DAISY
>   (whispers)
>   I thought so. You don't seem like
>   an old person... like my
>   grandma...

>   BENJAMIN
>   I'm not.

>   DAISY
>   Are you sick?

>   BENJAMIN
>   (whispers)
>   Well, I heard momma and Tizzy
>   whisper. They said I was going to
>   die soon.
>   (smiles)
>   But maybe not.

Daisy looks at him in the flickering candlelight.

>   DAISY
>   You're odd. You are different than
>   anybody I have ever met. May I?

>   BENJAMIN
>   Okay.

She innocently reaches to touch the skin on his cheek to
see what it feels like... When suddenly a sheet is pulled
back and Daisy's grandmother is standing there.

>   GRANDMA FULLER
>   What are you doing under there?

>   (CONTINUED)

Daisy blows out the candle and crawls quickly out from
the table.

> GRANDMA FULLER (CONT'D)
> You come right out here and get
> back up to bed...! It's after
> midnight!
> > (and for Benjamin,
> > but saying it to
> > Daisy)
> You are not to be playing
> together!

> DAISY
> Yes ma'am.

> GRANDMA FULLER
> > (moving her along)
> Now, you get back to bed, little
> lady...! You're too young to be
> wandering around in the night on
> your own...
> > (and a last word to
> > Benjamin)
> And you ought to be ashamed of
> yourself!

And they're gone... Benjamin left sitting alone under the
sheets. There's a slight sound and he sees Queenie, in
her nightgown, standing in the doorway...

> QUEENIE
> You are a different child... a man
> child, and baby, people aren't
> going to understand just how
> different you are.

> BENJAMIN
> > (forlorn)
> What's wrong with me, Momma?

> QUEENIE
> Come here.
> > (embracing him)
> God hasn't said yet baby. Now, go
> on to bed and behave yourself. Go
> on. Say your prayers, hear.

(CONTINUED)

61 INT. BEDROOM, NOLAN HOUSE - LATE NIGHT, 1930 61

Benjamin climbing back into bed. And Mr. Daws, unable to
sleep...

> MR. DAWS
> Did I ever tell you I've been
> struck by lightning seven times.
> Once, when I was repairing a leak
> on the roof.

And we see just that, the old man on a roof getting
blasted.

> MR. DAWS (CONT'D)
> Once, when I was just crossing the
> road getting the mail...

And we see that, the man peacefully crossing a country
road to get the mail, getting hit by lightning... But
Benjamin just sits there...he lies down turning his back
to the old man... all he can think about.... despite
everything...

> BENJAMIN BUTTON'S (V.O.)
> I never forgot her...

62 INT. THE HOSPITAL ROOM, NEW ORLEANS - DAY, PRESENT 62

The words linger. Daisy, her extraordinary blue eyes,
lying on her death bed... the rattle of the window in the
wind...

> CAROLINE
> (gently)
> ...blue eyes

> CAROLINE (CONT'D)
> Mom, did you get that this
> Benjamin loved you from the first
> time that he saw you.

She doesn't say anything.

(CONTINUED)

                        CAROLINE (CONT'D)
                Not many people experience that.

It's quiet.

                        CAROLINE (CONT'D)
                You want me to go on?

Daisy nods.

                        CAROLINE (CONT'D)
                He crosses something out...

                        BENJAMIN BUTTON'S (V.O.)
                "...When that baby came things
                were different..."

63   INT. THE KITCHEN, NOLAN HOUSE - NIGHT, 1931   63

We see Benjamin in his pajamas, quietly coming into the
kitchen for something to eat... And he slows, seeing
Queenie, taking a moment to herself, sitting at the
kitchen table, peacefully rocking and singing to her
infant... as Benjamin slips back out unseen.

64   INT. ATTIC, NOLAN HOUSE - NIGHT, 1931   64

We see Benjamin lying on a small bed in the ATTIC...
cluttered with years of accumulated things...

There's a noise. And we see Ngunda Oti is at the door, a
suitcase in hand.

                        NGUNDA OTI
                I've come to say goodbye. I'm
                going away.

                        BENJAMIN
                Going? Where?

                        NGUNDA OTI
                I haven't figured that out yet,
                but I'll send you a postcard when
                I get there.

                        BENJAMIN
                What about your friend? The tall
                lady?

                                        (CONTINUED)

                              NGUNDA OTI
                    We're not friends anymore. That's
                    what happens with tall people
                    sometimes.

                              BENJAMIN
                    Well...Goodbye...

And he's gone.   Benjamin gets up going to the window.
He looks outside.   He can see Mr. Oti come onto the
porch. There's a full moon.   And as he walks off, his
arrogant little walk, suitcase in hand, going out the
gate, Benjamin watches him disappear into the night.

                              BENJAMIN BUTTON'S (V.O.)
                    I spent a lot of time by myself
                    that year...

65   INT. FRONT ROOM, NOLAN HOUSE - ANOTHER DAY, 1931   65

Benjamin is lying on the front stairs playing with his
army men.

We see a refined, genteel OLD WOMAN, wearing a hat and
gloves, a suitcase at her feet, flanked by an old DOG,
just inside the front door...

                              THE WOMAN
                    Hello?...

                              BENJAMIN
                    Hi...

                              THE WOMAN
                    I'm moving in today.

And just then Queenie appears, the baby on her hip...

                              QUEENIE
                    Welcome... we've been expecting
                    you...
                         (to Benjamin)
                    Could you please show her up to
                    Mrs. Rousseau's old room?
                         (frowning)
                    I'm sorry but we usually don't
                    allow dogs in the house.

                                                      (CONTINUED)

                        THE WOMAN
               Well she's old as the hills.
               She's almost blind, she won't be a
               bother much longer.

Benjamin, like any young boy, immediately pets the old
dog...

                        QUEENIE
               Well alright as long as she stays
               from up underfoot.

Benjamin helps her with her bags showing her up the
stairs...the old dog dutifully following them...

                        BENJAMIN
               Right this way Mrs....

The woman starts to tell him her name... but we don't
hear it because...

                        BENJAMIN BUTTON'S (V.O.)
                   (after a beat)
               As hard as I try, I can't remember
               her name. Mrs. Lawson, Mrs.
               Hartford, or maybe it was Maple?
               It's funny how sometimes the
               people we remember the least, make
               the greatest impression on us.

66   INT. THE OLDER WOMAN'S ROOM, NOLAN HOUSE - DAY, 1931   66

Benjamin sits petting the dog while the Woman puts her
things away...

                        BENJAMIN BUTTON'S (V.O.)
               I do remember she wore diamonds...
               and she always dressed in fine
               clothing as if she was going out.
               Although, she never did and nobody
               ever came to visit her.

67   INT. NOLAN HOUSE, PARLOR - VISITING DAY, 1931   67

We see the Woman dressed nicely, sitting in a chair
reading a book. She takes a look out the window at the
families on the lawn and bends back to her book.

                                              (CONTINUED)

>   BENJAMIN BUTTON'S (V.O.)
>   ...She taught me how to play the
>   piano...

68   INT. PARLOR, NOLAN HOUSE - ANOTHER NIGHT, 1932   68

The Woman sitting with Benjamin teaching him how to play
piano...playing a classical piece like Chopin...Benjamin
trying his hand...sounding pretty bad...

>   THE WOMAN
>   It's not about how well you play,
>   it's how you feel about what you
>   play. (whispers) Try this.

And she plays a ragtime piece...New Orleans music...music
for the other whole part of the soul... Benjamin tries
his hand and actually plays it fairly well.

>   THE WOMAN (CONT'D)
>   You can't help putting yourself
>   into the music.

And he plays along with her...a piece he won't soon
forget...

>   BENJAMIN BUTTON'S (V.O.)
>   There were many changes, some you
>   could see... some you couldn't.

69   INT. A BATHROOM, NOLAN HOUSE - NIGHT, 1932   69

We see Benjamin taking a bath. An he notices a single
grey hair floating on the surface...

>   BENJAMIN BUTTON'S (V.O.)
>   Hair had started growing, in all
>   sorts of places...

And he sees some hair is under his arms... and as he
looks downward...

>   BENJAMIN BUTTON'S (V.O.) (CONT'D)
>   Along with other things...

Benjamin, naked, looking at himself in a mirror... like a
young teenage boy...

>   (CONTINUED)

                              BENJAMIN BUTTON'S (V.O.) (CONT'D)
                    I felt pretty good considering...

And as he flexes his muscles, feeling like a man.

70   INT. HOSPITAL ROOM, NEW ORLEANS - DAY, PRESENT   70

The wind blowing, splattering rain against the window.
Knocking.

                         DAISY
                      (in pain)
                  Oh, the pain...

                         CAROLINE
                  Alright Mom, I'll get the nurse...

She hurries out of the room. Daisy looks at the TV. A
weather map showing the big storm approaching. Caroline
comes back with a Nurse.

                         THE NURSE
                  Not doing too good?

She adjusts the morphine drip. Daisy lays back.

                         THE NURSE (CONT'D)
                  Nobody seems to know whether to
                  stay or leave. I'm gonna ride it
                  out.
                       (finishing with the
                        drip)
                  There, that should make things
                  much easier.
                       (turning to Caroline)
                  Have you had a chance to say your
                  goodbyes? My father waited four
                  hours for my brother to get here
                  from Boger City. He couldn't go
                  without him. She seems like a
                  sweet woman.

                         CAROLINE
                  Yeah. I haven't had as much time
                  with her...

Another NURSE looks in...

                                            (CONTINUED)

                              ANOTHER NURSE
                    You busy?

                              NURSE
                    Would you excuse me?

                              CAROLINE
                    Sure.

                              ANOTHER NURSE
                    I could use your help.

She leaves. Caroline sits back down. Daisy, starting to
feel the effects of the morphine...Caroline resumes
reading.

                              CAROLINE
                    "Queenie would let me go..."

                              BENJAMIN (V.O.)
                    ... with Mr Daws to Poverty
                    Point...To watch the boats go up
                    and down the river...

71   EXT. THE MISSISSIPPI RIVER - DAY, 1932   71

The busy docks... Men waiting, hoping to find work...

                              BENJAMIN BUTTON'S (V.O.)
                    These were hard times...

And we see Benjamin, with Mr. Daws, "the lightning man,"
sitting on a bench with a line of other old men, "killing
time," watching the boats going up and down the River...

                              MR. DAWS
                    Did I ever tell you I was struck
                    by lightning seven times? Once,
                    when I was in a field just tending
                    to my cows.

And we see just that, Mr. Daws, along with a cow of his,
being hit by lightning.

                                                 (CONTINUED)

                        A MAN'S (V.O.)
                    (shouts)
              My fourt' hand didn't show up...
              Anybody want to make $2 for a
              day's work around here...

Benjamin turns... And he sees a man in his late 40s,
standing on the dock in front of a TUGBOAT, an old rusted
tug built out of charcoal iron... The man, its Captain
MIKE... Has a thick Irish accent... For some reason none
of the able-bodied men needing work respond...

                        CAPT. MIKE
              What's the matter? Nobody wants to
              do an honest day's work for an
              honest day's pay...!

                        A MAN
                    (warning them)
              He never pays...

                        CAPT. MIKE
              Nobody wants a job?

Benjamin suddenly springs up at the opportunity, waving
his arms...

                        BENJAMIN
              I do...!

                        CAPT. MIKE
              You got your sea legs about you
              old man?

                        BENJAMIN
                    (feeling his legs)
              I do. I think.

                        CAPT. MIKE
              Well that's good enough for me!
              Get your ass on board, we'll sure
              as hell find out!

And as Benjamin gets on the boat, heading out to sea...

EXT. TUGBOAT, MISSISSIPPI RIVER, NEW ORLEANS - DAY, 1932

And we see Benjamin "learning the ropes..." Helping to
tow the freighters, into and out of the River ports...
Benjamin in this element, like a boy, his hair blowing,
thrilled to be on the boat, thrilled by the adventure...
willing to do anything...

> BENJAMIN BUTTON'S (V.O.)
> I was as happy as I could be... I
> would do anything...

> CAPT. MIKE
> I needs a volunteah.

> BENJAMIN
> Yes, Captain!

> CAPT. MIKE
> (motioning)
> Scrape off all this bird shit.

> BENJAMIN
> Right away, sir...!

And he hops to it... Happily scraping off the bird
shit... Happy to be doing anything...

> BENJAMIN BUTTON'S (V.O.)
> And I was actually going to be
> paid for something I would have
> done for free.

> BENJAMIN BUTTON'S (V.O.) (CONT'D)
> His name was Captain Mike Clark...
> He'd been on a tugboat since he
> was seven...

73   INT. TUGBOAT WHEELHOUSE - END OF ANOTHER DAY, 1932   73

Mike's a hard drinker, God's last angry man... He's
drinking as they go in for the night... Benjamin sitting
with him in the wheelhouse... Capt. Mike jawing away...

> CAPT. MIKE
> Can you still get it up?

(CONTINUED)

                              BENJAMIN
                         (doesn't understand)
                    I do every morning.

                              CAPT. MIKE
                    The old pole? The high hard'n?

                              BENJAMIN
                         (not so sure)
                    I guess.

                              CAPT. MIKE
                    When was the last time you had a
                    woman...?

                              BENJAMIN
                    Never.

                              CAPT. MIKE
                    Never!

                              BENJAMIN
                    Not that I know of sir.

                              CAPT. MIKE
                         (can't believe his
                          ears)
                    Wait a minute. You mean to say you
                    been on this earth for however
                    many years and you've never had a
                    woman?!

Benjamin shakes his head.

                              CAPT. MIKE (CONT'D)
                    That's the saddest thing I ever
                    heard in my life. Never?

                              BENJAMIN
                    Nope.

                              CAPT. MIKE
                    Well, then, by Jesus, you're
                    comin' with me!!

                              BENJAMIN BUTTON'S (V.O.)
                    He took me to meet some friends...

Music playing loud... We see Benjamin and Capt. Mike at
the bar... Mike, hammered...

> CAPT. MIKE
> What did your father do?

> BENJAMIN
> I never met my father.

> CAPT. MIKE
> You're a lucky bastard! All
> fathers want to do is hold you
> down!.. Out on my father's boat,
> working da two-a-days... This
> littl' fat bastard, "tug Irish,"
> what they calls them. I fin'ly
> get up the nerves and tell him...
> "I don't wanta spend da rest of my
> life on a goddamn tugboat...!" You
> know what I'm sayin'?

> BENJAMIN
> You didn't want to spend the rest
> of your life on a tugboat.

> CAPT. MIKE
> Absolutely, damn right! So you
> know what my father says to me?
> He says "Who the hell you think
> you are?" "What the hell you
> think you can do?" I tell him.
> "Well if you askin' -- I want to
> be a artist." He laughs. "An
> artist? God wanted you to work a
> tugboat just like me, and that's
> what you goin' to do?" I turned
> myself into an artist...

And he suddenly takes off his shirt, pulls down his
pants... And we see he's covered, from head to toe, with
"his artwork," and incredible array of tattoos...

> CAPT. MIKE (CONT'D)
> A tattoo artist...! I puts on
> every one of these myself!

(CONTINUED)

And they look it, upside down, sideways, and backwards...

                    CAPT. MIKE (CONT'D)
           You have to skin me alive to take
           my art away from me now! When I'm
           dead I'm going to send him my arm!
           Don't let anyone tell you
           different! You got to do what you
           meant to do! And I happen to be a
           god-damned artist!

                    BENJAMIN
           (stating the obvious)
           But you're a tugboat captain.

Which stops Captain Mike in mid rant... And he has no
answer for... His only response is to glare at
Benjamin... A back door opens, a slinky woman coming
in...

                    THE WOMAN
           Captain Mike, we're ready for you
           and your friend...

                    CAPT. MIKE
           Let's go old timer... Break your
           cherry...

75   INT. WHORE HOUSE, THE QUARTER, NEW ORLEANS - NIGHT, 1932   **75**

Captain Mike and Benjamin in a small parlor where girls,
both black and white, are lining the stairs....

                    CAPT. MIKE
           Hello my lovelies.

                    GIRLS
           Hello Captain Mike.

Benjamin removes his hat.

                    BENJAMIN
           Hi.

Benjamin left standing, not knowing what to do... None of
the women seem too anxious to be with the old man...

                                  (CONTINUED)

                              ONE OF THE WOMEN
                        He gives me the willies, he's not
                        for me....

A thin Girl, maybe 19, of mixed ethnicity, decides to
take a chance...

                              THE GIRL
                        How are you tonight, Grandpa?

                              BENJAMIN BUTTON'S (V.O.)
                        It was a night to remember...

76   OMITTED   **76**

76A   OMITTED   **76A**

77   INT. THE ROOM, WHORE HOUSE, FRENCH QUARTER - NIGHT, 1932   **77**

We see the covers moving. Benjamin and the girl are going
at it. The girl sticks her head out and looks at the
clock.

                              THE GIRL
                        What are you, Dick Tracy or
                        something? I've got to rest...

And that's just what she's doing... trying to catch her
breath...

                              BENJAMIN
                            (in heaven)
                        Again?

78   INT. PARLOR, WHORE HOUSE, THE QUARTER - LATER STILL, 1932   **78**

And we see Benjamin, at the door, happily smiling...

                              BENJAMIN
                        Thank you...

                              THE GIRL
                            (hurting)
                        No, thank you...

Benjamin, floating on air, hovering, never wants to
leave...

                                              (CONTINUED)

                                THE GIRL (CONT'D)
                        Have a nice night...

                                BENJAMIN
                        Will you be here tomorrow?

                                THE GIRL
                        Every night, but Sunday...

And she's finally able to go...

                                BENJAMIN BUTTON'S (V.O.)
                        It sure made me understand the
                        value of earning a living... the
                        things it can buy you..

Benjamin turns to leave... we hear footsteps... And we
see a man, putting on a raincoat, coming downstairs from
one of those other rooms... We see it's Benjamin's
father... THOMAS BUTTON... Seeing Benjamin he slows...
Benjamin, unaware of who he is, turns and goes out...

79   EXT. STREET, FRENCH QUARTER - LATE AT NIGHT, 1932   79

It's a rainy night. Benjamin, feeling like a million
bucks, walks along the street, going home... A
chauffeured car pulls alongside him, the window rolled
down... And we see Thomas Button in the car...

                                THOMAS BUTTON
                        It's nasty out. Can I offer you a
                        ride somewhere...?

                                BENJAMIN
                        That's awfully kind of you, sir.

He gets into the car.

80   INT. THOMAS' CAR, NEW ORLEANS - LATE AT NIGHT, 1932   80

They drive in awkward silence.

                                THOMAS BUTTON
                        My name is Thomas, Thomas Button.

                                BENJAMIN
                        I'm Benjamin.

                                                    (CONTINUED)

> THOMAS BUTTON
>   (saying the name to
>   himself)
> Benjamin... It's a pleasure to
> know you.

They shake hands.

> THOMAS BUTTON (CONT'D)
> Would you like to stop somewhere
> and have a drink?

81   INT. BAR, FRENCH QUARTER - LATE AT NIGHT, 1932   81

A small old bar. Benjamin and his father sitting in the
back... The waiter comes over, deferring to Benjamin's
age...

> THE WAITER
> What will it be sir?

> BENJAMIN
> I'll have whatever he's having.

> THOMAS BUTTON
> A Sazerac for both of us...with
> whiskey instead of brandy...

The waiter leaves.

> THOMAS BUTTON (CONT'D)
> You don't drink do you?

> BENJAMIN
> It's a night for firsts...

> THOMAS BUTTON
> How is that?

> BENJAMIN
> I've never been to a brothel
> either.

> THOMAS BUTTON
> It's an... experience...

> BENJAMIN
> It certainly is.

(CONTINUED)

                    BENJAMIN (CONT'D)
          There's a time for everything.

                    THOMAS BUTTON
          True enough. I don't mean to be
          rude... but your hands...is that
          painful?

                    BENJAMIN
          I was born with some form of a
          disease.

                    THOMAS BUTTON
          What kind of a disease?

                    BENJAMIN
          I was born old.

Thomas is quiet. And for many things...

                    THOMAS BUTTON
          I'm sorry.

                    BENJAMIN
               (guileless)
          No need to be. Nothing wrong with
          old age.

Thomas looks at him... They get their drinks... Tap
glasses, and drink. Benjamin coughs at the taste... But
forces it down... And as they laugh at his discomfort...

82   INT. THE BAR - FRENCH QUARTER - LATER THAT NIGHT, 1932   82

Thomas and Benjamin deep in conversation... and both of
them more than a few sheets to the wind... Benjamin,
particularly overblown like any first time drunk...

                    THOMAS BUTTON
          ... My wife passed away many years
          ago...

                    BENJAMIN
               (slurring)
          I'm so so sorry.

                    THOMAS BUTTON
          She died in childbirth.

                                        (CONTINUED)

And there's a moment when it seems like Thomas might tell
him, but despite the alcohol he thinks better of it...

>   THOMAS BUTTON (CONT'D)
>   (toasts, sadly)
>   To children.

>   BENJAMIN
>   (nods, toasts)
>   To mothers...

After some moments:

>   BENJAMIN (CONT'D)
>   What line of work are you in, Mr.
>   Button?

>   THOMAS BUTTON
>   Buttons. "Button's Buttons."
>   There isn't a button we don't
>   make. Our biggest competition is
>   B.F. Goodrich and his infernal
>   zippers...

The waiter comes over.

>   THE WAITER
>   Would you gentlemen like anything
>   else?

>   THOMAS BUTTON
>   One for the road Benjamin?

>   BENJAMIN
>   Only if you'll let me pay for it,
>   Mr. Button...

He takes out a little of his hard earned pay... proud of
himself...

>   THOMAS BUTTON
>   What line of work do you do?

>   BENJAMIN
>   (proud of himself)
>   I'm a tugboat man.

EXT. NOLAN HOUSE - LATE AT NIGHT, 1932

The car's stopped outside the gate... Benjamin is
drunkenly getting out...

> THOMAS BUTTON
> I enjoyed talking to you...

> BENJAMIN
> I enjoyed drinking with you...

He starts to wobble inside...

> THOMAS BUTTON
> (after him)
> Benjamin...

Benjamin slows...

> THOMAS BUTTON (CONT'D)
> Would you mind, if time to time, I
> stopped by to say hello...?

> BENJAMIN
> (a drunken wave)
> Anytime. Goodnight Mr. Button.

> THOMAS BUTTON
> (happily)
> Goodnight, Benjamin.

Benjamin turns inside. Thomas looks after him for a long
moment... And then he drives away...

INT. NOLAN HOUSE - LATE NIGHT, 1932

Benjamin holding the railing for support starts up the
stairs for bed.

> QUEENIE'S (V.O.)
> Where have you been!?

And we see Queenie has been sitting in the front room...
where she can see out the window...

> BENJAMIN
> Nothing I met some people and
> listened to some music.... I --

(CONTINUED)

He doesn't mention the whore... And right on cue
Benjamin, wobbles...And to finish the evening, he throws
up.

85   EXT. LAWN, NOLAN HOUSE - ANOTHER DAY, 1934   85

The family's on the lawn...

> BENJAMIN BUTTON'S (V.O.)
> Growing up's a funny thing. It
> sneaks up on you. One person is
> there and suddenly somebody else
> has taken her place. She wasn't
> all elbows and knees anymore.

Daisy runs up to Benjamin who is sitting in a chair in
the sun.

> DAISY
> Benjamin, come on.

> BENJAMIN
> Okay.

He stands slowly and follows her.

> BENJAMIN BUTTON'S (V.O.)
> I loved those weekends when she
> would come and spend the night
> with her grandma.

86   INT. GRANDMA FULLER'S ROOM - DAWN, 1934   86

Daisy, 9 now, asleep in bed with Grandma Fuller... We see
Benjamin quietly enter... He gently nudges Daisy awake...

> BENJAMIN
> (whispers)
> Daisy. Daisy. Do you want to see
> something? You got to keep it a
> secret.

Daisy, always willing, always brave, gets up...

> BENJAMIN (CONT'D)
> (whispers)
> Get dressed. I'll meet you out
> back...

And he leaves the room as quickly as he came...

87   EXT. BEHIND THE KITCHEN - NOLAN HOUSE - DAWN, 1934   87

Benjamin, in an old peacoat, holding another -- waits...
Daisy comes out... as he stops the door from slamming...

                    BENJAMIN
        Ssssh...Come on.
              (whispers)
        Can you swim?

                    DAISY
        I can do anything you can do...

                    BENJAMIN
        Here, put this on...

He gives her a heavy coat...she puts it on... It's two
sizes too big for her...

                    BENJAMIN (CONT'D)
        We have to hurry...

And she follows him across the yard... the two of them
going quickly down the street...

88   EXT. THE DOCKS, MISSISSIPPI RIVER - DAYBREAK, 1934   88

Fog. The first light of dawn. A full compliment of
boats tied up for the night... They scamper along the
dock... to the "Chelsea" ...Benjamin helps her climb
aboard...

89   INT. TUGBOAT, MISSISSIPPI RIVER - DAYBREAK, 1934   89

He goes upstairs to find -- Captain Mike sprawled across
his bunk -- in all his naked tattooed glory, an empty
bottle on the floor...

                    DAISY
        Is he okay?

                    BENJAMIN
             (shaking him)
        Captain. Captain Mike... Morning
        Captain. Can you take us out?

                        (CONTINUED)

Captain Mike opens one eye... sees them standing there...

> CAPT. MIKE
> You know what day it is?

> BENJAMIN
> Sunday.

> CAPT. MIKE
> Do you know what dat mean?

He doesn't.

> CAPT. MIKE (CONT'D)
> It means I was very drunk last
> night.

> BENJAMIN
> You're drunk every night.

Captain Mike just squints.

> CAPT. MIKE
> Is that a girl?

> BENJAMIN
> A close friend... I wanted to show
> her the River.

> CAPT. MIKE
> I'm not supposed to be joy-ridin'
> with civilians... I could lose my
> license.

That notion stops him for about a nanosecond. He sits up.

> CAPT. MIKE (CONT'D)
> (grabbing a bottle)
> What are you waitin' for!

90   EXT. THE TUGBOAT, THE MISSISSIPPI RIVER - EARLY, 1934   90

The tugboat making its way through the fog... Benjamin
standing with Daisy on the prow... the wind in their
faces... And suddenly out of the fog a HORN BLARES... As
loud as anything they have ever heard... and moving out
of the mist, horn still echoing, a huge ocean liner
appears... With three other tugboats pushing it to sea...

(CONTINUED)

                          CAPT. MIKE
                 She put in for repair... a wounded
                 duck... She's flyin' now...

Captain Mike joins the tugs at the liner's side... the
tugs sounding horns of their own... a symphony of a
kind... What interests Benjamin...

Passengers line the railing... continuing their
adventure... And what interests Daisy...

Daisy, thrilled, waves to them -- the passengers along
the rail, waving back... Benjamin stands by Daisy, their
hair blowing in the salty air....

                          DAISY
                      (to Benjamin)
                 I wish we could go with them...

As they watch the liner, like a foggy dream, sailing
away...

91   INT. THE HOSPITAL ROOM, NEW ORLEANS - DAY, PRESENT   91

The rain and wind knocking at the window...

                          CAROLINE
                 Did you say something, Mom?

Daisy doesn't say anything. Caroline worriedly looks out
the window.

                      CAROLINE (CONT'D)
                 It's getting really bad. Can you
                 hear me Momma? Huh?

                          DAISY
                 ... time has just seeped out of
                 me...

                          CAROLINE
                      (after a beat)
                 "Things were changing quickly."

92   INT. UPSTAIRS BATHROOM - NOLAN HOUSE - ANOTHER DAY, 1935   92

We see Benjamin's REFLECTION in a mirror... WE PULL BACK
TO SEE we're in the bathroom...

                                              (CONTINUED)

Benjamin sitting in a straight back chair... getting a
haircut... the dog at their feet...

                    THE WOMAN
          I don't know how it's possible,
          you seem to have more hair...

                    BENJAMIN
               (a little arrogant)
          What if I told you that I wasn't
          getting older -- I was getting
          younger than everybody else...

And she then says, taking the wind out of his sails...

                    THE WOMAN
          Well, I'd feel sorry for you... to
          have to see everybody you love,
          die before you.

He's quiet, he hadn't thought of that...

                    THE WOMAN (CONT'D)
          It's an awful responsibility...

                    BENJAMIN BUTTON'S (V.O.)
          I had never thought about life or
          death that way before...

He's still... And seeing he's upset, she says the most
beautiful of things...

                    THE WOMAN
          Benjamin... We're meant to lose
          the people we love. How else
          would we know how important they
          are to us.

                    BENJAMIN BUTTON'S (V.O.)
          And one fall day... a familiar
          visitor came knocking on our
          door...

93   INT. NOLAN HOUSE - ANOTHER DAY, 1936   93

We see Benjamin looking through the Woman's door...

                                                    (CONTINUED)

                          BENJAMIN
                You want to go with me to the drug
                store?

There's no response. He opens it, going inside... The
Woman is sitting in a chair by the window, the dog at her
feet, the familiar Victrola playing dance music... He
comes around the chair. And he sees she's still...
perfectly still... her soul moved on...

94   EXT. CEMETERY PLOT, NEW ORLEANS CEMETERY - DAY, 1936   94

We see an old New Orleans paupers' cemetery... Benjamin
and the mourners, and because he can't remember her name,
around an unmarked grave...

                          BENJAMIN BUTTON'S (V.O.)
                She taught me how to play the
                piano.

As Benjamin watches the woman go to her final rest.

                          BENJAMIN BUTTON'S (V.O.) (CONT'D)
                And she taught me what it meant to
                miss somebody.

95   INT. BENJAMIN'S ROOM, ATTIC - NOLAN HOUSE - DAY, 1936   95

We see Benjamin taking some things out of a dresser
drawer, packing a suitcase...

                          BENJAMIN BUTTON'S (V.O.)
                I had gone to a brothel, I'd had
                my first drink, I had said goodbye
                to one friend and buried
                another... In 1936, when I was
                coming to the end of the 17th year
                of my life, I packed my bag...

We see him putting some final things into the suitcase,
closing it...

                          BENJAMIN BUTTON'S (V.O.) (CONT'D)
                ...and said goodbye...

INT. PARLOR, NOLAN HOUSE, NEW ORLEANS - DAY, 1936

We see Benjamin moving through the parlor, one by one, saying his goodbyes to the old people...

>   BENJAMIN BUTTON'S (V.O.)
>   I knew, life being what it was, I
>   would probably never see them
>   again...

The familiar faces... And as we watch him affectionately touch or talk to each of them... we can see DAISY, almost thirteen now, leaning against the corner of the hall... Out of sight... as if she didn't say goodbye, he wouldn't leave...

EXT. THE FRONT PORCH - NOLAN HOUSE - DAY, 1936

We see TIZZY on the porch holding Benjamin's suitcase for him... The woman's old dog lying beside him...

>   TIZZY
>   (shaking his hand)
>   Good luck to you, son.

And we see Queenie has come out onto the porch and he holds Queenie... tears running down her face...

>   BENJAMIN
>   I love you Momma...

>   QUEENIE
>   I love you too baby. I want you to
>   say your prayers every night, you
>   hear? Be safe.

He takes up his suitcase and starts off the porch... going down the walkway... he hesitates, and opens the gate... moving out onto the street... When suddenly Daisy is calling him...

>   DAISY
>   Benjamin...

She comes running. He stops to let her catch up to him...

                                                  (CONTINUED)

                        DAISY (CONT'D)
          Where are you going?

                        BENJAMIN
          To sea. I'll send you a postcard.

                        DAISY
          From everywhere. Write me a
          postcard from everywhere...

And with so much she wants to say, she can't say
anything. So she runs away... He watches her go, watches
her thin legs running back down the street... and he
turns and moves off along the street...

We see him in the distance, the "old man", a 17 year old,
suitcase in hand, going to find out who he is and what he
is to become...

98   INT. HOSPITAL, NEW ORLEANS - DAY, THE PRESENT   98

Caroline opens a wooden cigar box...It's filled with
postcards... going through them...

                        DAISY
              Can you imagine.... He sent me a
              postcard from everywhere he went...
              every place he worked...
              Newfoundland... Baffin Bay...
              Liverpool, Glasgow, Narvik. He had
              gone with that Captain Mike.

99   EXT. SOMEWHERE ON THE SEA - DAY, 1937   99

The Tugboat, in the distance, steaming through the
ocean...

                        BENJAMIN BUTTON'S (V.O.)
              Captain Mike had contracted for
              three years with Moran Brothers
              Tug and Salvage... The old ship
              had been refitted with a diesel
              engine, and a new sea winch... We
              went around Florida and up the
              Atlantic seaboard...

EXT. TUGBOAT, AT SEA - DAY, 1937

The refitted "Chelsea" on the Atlantic Ocean...

                    BENJAMIN BUTTON'S (V.O.)
                We were a crew of seven now...
                Captain Mike and me... the
                Cookie... Prentiss Mayes from
                Wilmington, Delaware...

And we see an old sea hand in his domain, his GALLEY,
smoking and coughing as he cooks...

                    BENJAMIN BUTTON'S (V.O.) (CONT'D)
                ...The Brody twins... Rick and
                Vic...

Two burly hard working IDENTICAL TWIN BROTHERS...

                    BENJAMIN BUTTON'S (V.O.) (CONT'D)
                Who got along fine at sea... but
                for some reason, once they were on
                dry land... couldn't stand the
                sight of each other...

101   EXT. DOCK SOMEWHERE - DAY, 1937   101

The brothers getting off the tug... and no sooner have
they hit dry land they immediately get into a fist
fight...

102   EXT. TUGBOAT, AT SEA — DUSK, 1937   102

We see a dour looking man... who always expects the
worst...

                JOHN GRIMM
            You know one in every eight boats
            never returns.

                    BENJAMIN BUTTON'S (V.O.)
            There was John Grimm, who sure fit
            his name...

                JOHN GRIMM
            ...all hands lost at sea.

                                    (CONTINUED)

                              BENJAMIN BUTTON'S (V.O.)
                    ...from Belvedere, South Dakota...

                              BENJAMIN BUTTON'S (V.O.) (CONT'D)
                    ...and Pleasant Curtis from
                    Nashville, who never said a word
                    to anyone... except to himself...

The asocial Pleasant... talking to himself as he works...

103   EXT. ATLANTIC OCEAN - DAY, 1938   103

Benjamin standing on the bow of the old tug as it sloughs
through a fog on the high seas... ready to see the world.

104   INT. HOSPITAL ROOM, NEW ORLEANS - DAY, PRESENT   104

Daisy lying in bed...

                              DAISY
                    I wrote him constantly....

105   EXT. HARBOR SOMEWHERE - NIGHTFALL, 1938   105

The tug on its way in for the night... Benjamin, sitting
on a cleat, reading her letter...

                              DAISY'S (V.O.)
                    ...I told him I had been invited
                    to audition in New York City for
                    the School of American Ballet...

106   EXT. NEW YORK SKYLINE - DAY, 1938   106

Tilting from the grey sky, onto an old landmark building.

107   INT. LANDMARK BUILDING, DANCE LOFT, NEW YORK - DAY, 1938   107

A large open DANCE LOFT. And we see Daisy, dancing for a
selection committee seated on metal chairs... Daisy
moving with technical proficiency -- but it's bloodless,
without any real distinction... She gets nods -- but no
kudos...

                              DAISY'S (V.O.)
                    I was relegated to the "corps"...
                    another dancing gypsy...

                                                  (CONTINUED)

We see Daisy training... just another lithe body.

108-110 OMITTED   **108-110**

111   EXT. MURMANSK HARBOR, RUSSIA - DAY, 1941   **111**

We see "Chelsea" working with other tugs as snow falls in
the crowded Russian Harbor.

                    CAPT. MIKE
              Benjamin...

Benjamin, who is coiling rope on the bow, stands and
looks at the Captain.

                    CAPT. MIKE (CONT'D)
                 (squinting down at
                  him, wanting to
                  know)
              How's it when you showed up you
              were no bigger than a bollard with
              one foot in the grave. Now either
              I drink a helluva lot more than I
              think I do, or you sprouted...
              What's your secret?

And Benjamin, tired of explanations, and what comes first
to mind...

                    BENJAMIN
              Well Captain, you do drink a lot.

And that makes perfect sense to Mike...

And Benjamin stands on the bow...ready to see the
world...

                    BENJAMIN BUTTON'S (V.O.)

              We stayed at a small hotel with a
              grand name, "The Winter Palace."

112   EXT. MURMANSK STREET, RUSSIA - NIGHT, 1941   112

Snow covers the street outside of a turn-of-the Century
hotel... a front window looks into its lobby... "The
Winter Palace Hotel."

113   INT. "WINTER PALACE," RUSSIA - NIGHT, 1941   113

There's a packed BAR off the lobby... We see Benjamin
sitting with Captain Mike, their crew, and a mixture of
other seamen, Russians and other ethnics, all speaking
different languages, sitting and standing around tables
cluttered with bottles and glasses... Captain Mike,
drunk, his shirt off, is telling a Russian sailor,
another interpreting for him -- about a tattoo he has
over his heart... an upside down hummingbird...

> CAPT. MIKE
> The hummingbird is not just anoter
> bird! Its heart rate's twelve
> hunerd beats a minute...! Its
> wings beats eighty times a
> second...! If you was to stop
> their wings from beatin, they
> would be dead' in less than ten
> seconds...This is no ordinary
> bird, this is a frikkin' miracle!
> They slowed down the wings
> wit' movin' pictures, you know
> what they saw, they wing tips are
> doin' dis...

And he draws on a napkin a FIGURE EIGHT...

> CAPT. MIKE (CONT'D)
> Do you know what the figure eight
> is the mathematical symbol
> for...?!

Pointing at the symbol...

> CAPT. MIKE (CONT'D)
> Infinity!

And for some drunken reason, no matter what language they
might speak, they all laugh...

(CONTINUED)

                              BENJAMIN BUTTON'S (V.O.)
                    Everybody, no matter what
                    differences they had, the
                    languages, the color of their
                    skin, had one thing in common...
                    they were drunk every single
                    night...

Then there's a shout -- and as if to underscore things,
the Brody twins are kicking the shit out of each other
again...

114   INT. LOBBY, "WINTER PALACE," RUSSIA - NIGHT, 1941   **114**

We see Benjamin waiting for the small caged elevator to
take him to his room. He gets in, the elevator operator
about to shut the grill door...

                              A WOMAN'S (V.O.)
                    Would you wait, please...

And we see a WOMAN in her late 40s... getting on the
elevator... Benjamin looks over at her...

                              BENJAMIN BUTTON'S (V.O.)
                    Her name was Elizabeth Abbott. She
                    was not beautiful. She was plain
                    as paper... But she was as pretty
                    as any picture to me...

"Plain as paper," ELIZABETH ABBOTT... Directly behind her
walks a tall, tired man, in his 50s... By the look of his
ruddy face, and her silent mien... they're both drunk...
Benjamin finds himself looking at her...

                              ELIZABETH ABBOTT
                    What are you looking at?

She has a distinctly English accent. Benjamin doesn't say
a word.

                              ELIZABETH ABBOTT (CONT'D)
                    If you must know, we have a long
                    standing agreement never to go to
                    bed sober. Isn't that right
                    darling?

                                                      (CONTINUED)

                         WALTER ABBOTT
              Whatever you say darling?

                         BENJAMIN BUTTON'S (V.O.)
                    Her husband was Walter Abbott...He
                    was Chief Minister of the British
                    Trade Mission in Murmansk... and
                    he was a spy...

They ride up. Elizabeth has her shoes off...She sees him
noting her stocking feet... The elevator finally rattles
to a stop, and Walter and Elizabeth get off... Starting
down the hall...she abruptly turns to say to Benjamin...
so that it's completely understood...

                         ELIZABETH ABBOTT
                    I broke the heel off of one of my
                    shoes...I'm not in the habit of
                    walking about in my stocking
                    feet...

And as he watches her saunter along the hallway... the
way drunks do... endeavoring to keep her dignity...

                         BENJAMIN BUTTON'S (V.O.)
                    They were long days there...

115   EXT. MURMANSK HARBOR, RUSSIA - DAY, 1941   115

Benjamin on the tug, but it's less fun now, not much
adventure, just hard work... Fighting the snow and the
wind, they tow a large freighter into port...

116   INT. BENJAMIN'S ROOM - "WINTER PALACE" - NIGHT, 1941   116

Benjamin, in his small room, cold air blasting through
the windows, looking out the window into the snowy
night...

                         BENJAMIN BUTTON'S (V.O.)
                    And even longer nights...

He lays on his bed looking out at the dark sky... the
snow falling...

                         BENJAMIN BUTTON'S (V.O.)
                    One particular night...I was
                    having trouble sleeping...

Benjamin trudges down the stairs, stepping tentatively
into the empty lobby... He slows, seeing ELIZABETH ABBOTT
in her bathrobe, sitting, alone and lonely... and it's
not the first time for her...

>   BENJAMIN
>   I'm sorry... I couldn't sleep...

She's quiet... She finally looks up... but doesn't say
anything... There's an awkward moment...exacerbated by
the stillness of the hotel in the middle of the night...

>   BENJAMIN (CONT'D)
>   I was going to make some
>   tea...would you like some?

>   ELIZABETH ABBOTT
>   Oh, no thank you.

She shakes her head no... He crosses through the empty
bar, into an old KITCHEN... He looks for tea... Puts
water in a kettle... As he watches the kettle boil...
Elizabeth, her arms folded across her chest as if she
were chilled, stands by the door... Benjamin, without
asking, takes a cup for her...

>   BENJAMIN
>   Milk...? Honey...?

>   ELIZABETH ABBOTT
>   Honey, please.

He finds a large honey jar... and seeing some dead flies
in with the sweet syrup he asks...

>   BENJAMIN
>   Hope you like flies in your honey.

>   ELIZABETH ABBOTT
>   Oh, perhaps not.

She smiles...for the first time... A thin smile... They
cross to the table...she sits...and he starts to pour the
tea... Elizabeth stopping him...

                                        (CONTINUED)

                              ELIZABETH ABBOTT (CONT'D)
                    Oh, maybe... you should let it
                    steep a little...

                              BENJAMIN
                    Steep?

                              ELIZABETH ABBOTT
                    Um...Soak. I don't know, I mean,
                    there's a proper way of making
                    tea.

                              BENJAMIN
                    Well, where I'm from, people just
                    want it to be hot.

                              ELIZABETH ABBOTT
                    Well...quite right.

She doesn't smile. They're quiet...two strangers... After
some moments...

                              ELIZABETH ABBOTT (CONT'D)
                    Now you're a seaman?

                              BENJAMIN
                    Sailor.

                              ELIZABETH ABBOTT
                    I hope you won't think me impolite
                    but I have to ask, aren't you a
                    little old to be working on a
                    boat?

                              BENJAMIN
                    There's no age limit... as long as
                    you can do the work...

She nods... Benjamin looks in the kettle and decides to
pour the tea.

                              ELIZABETH ABBOTT
                    And you have trouble sleeping?

                              BENJAMIN
                    I didn't think I did... I usually
                    sleep like a baby. Something's
                    been keeping me up.

                                             (CONTINUED)

                    ELIZABETH ABBOTT
          My father, in his eighties, he was
          so convinced he was going to die
          in his sleep...he limited himself
          to take afternoon naps...He was so
          determined he was going to cheat
          death.

                    BENJAMIN
          Did he?

                    ELIZABETH ABBOTT
          Did he what?

                    BENJAMIN
          Die in his sleep?

                    ELIZABETH ABBOTT
          He died sitting in his favorite
          chair listening to his favorite
          program on the wireless.

                    BENJAMIN
               (smiles)
          He must have known something.

She smiles at the idea... Another one... that goes as
quickly as it's come... And it's quiet again...

                    ELIZABETH ABBOTT
          My husband's the British Trade
          Minister and we've been here for
          fourteen months...

                    BENJAMIN
          Good God.

                    ELIZABETH ABBOTT
          We were supposed to go to
          Peking... but it never seemed to
          work out. Have you been in the Far
          East?

                    BENJAMIN
          No, I've never been anywhere
          really. I mean outside of harbors.

                                        (CONTINUED)

                              ELIZABETH ABBOTT
                     And where is it that you are from?

                              BENJAMIN
                     New Orleans, Louisiana.

                              ELIZABETH ABBOTT
                        (pure Elizabeth)
                     I didn't know there was another.

Which escapes him.

                              BENJAMIN BUTTON'S (V.O.)
                     And she told me about all the
                     places she had been, and what she
                     had seen...And we talked until
                     just before the dawn...

118   INT. KITCHEN, "WINTER PALACE," RUSSIA - DAYBREAK, 1941   **118**

The first hint of daylight...

She leaves as quietly as she entered... Benjamin remains
sitting for a moment...

                              BENJAMIN BUTTON'S (V.O.)
                     ...Then we went back to our
                     rooms... to our separate lives...

And as she goes back up the quiet stairs...

                              BENJAMIN BUTTON'S (V.O.) (CONT'D)
                     But every night... we would meet
                     again in that lobby...

119   INT. LOBBY, "WINTER PALACE," RUSSIA - DEAD OF NIGHT, 1941 **119**

Benjamin padding downstairs... slowing... happy to see
Elizabeth, in her bathrobe, sitting in the empty lobby,
waiting for him...

120   INT. KITCHEN, "WINTER PALACE," RUSSIA - BEFORE DAWN, 1941 **120**

Elizabeth and Benjamin quietly talking...

                              BENJAMIN BUTTON'S (V.O.)
                     A hotel in the middle of the night
                     can be a magical place...

                                                       (CONTINUED)

And we see the empty front desk and tiny silver bell...
The vacant lobby, with its musty old rugs... The open
elevator, waiting... The dining room, with its crisp
white tablecloths.

> BENJAMIN BUTTON'S (V.O.) (CONT'D)
> A mouse running and stopping...

A mouse crossing the lobby floor doing just that...

> BENJAMIN BUTTON'S (V.O.) (CONT'D)
> A radiator hissing. A curtain
> blowing.

We see and hear it all... All the little sounds, a
symphony, that make up life in a hotel in the middle of
the night... Benjamin and Elizabeth sitting quietly
drinking their tea.

> BENJAMIN BUTTON'S (V.O.) (CONT'D)
> There is something peaceful, even
> comforting, knowing that people
> you love are asleep in their beds,
> where nothing can harm them...

121   INT. VARIOUS BEDROOMS - DEAD OF NIGHT, 1941   121

Queenie and Tizzy asleep together in her bed... Their
child on the floor...Ngunda Oti asleep in a room
somewhere. And of course Daisy, in a New York apartment
loft with other dancers... sleeping peacefully.

> BENJAMIN BUTTON'S (V.O.)
> Elizabeth and I would loose track
> of the night until just before
> daybreak...

122   INT. KITCHEN - "WINTER PALACE" - RUSSIA - DAYBREAK, 1941   122

Daylight starts to creep in... she gets up, about to
go... she slows...

> ELIZABETH ABBOTT
> I think I may have given you the
> wrong impression.

> BENJAMIN
> Beg pardon?

                                                   (CONTINUED)

> ELIZABETH ABBOTT
> Well married women don't
> customarily sit around in the
> middle of the night with strange
> men in hotels.

> BENJAMIN
> (honestly)
> I wouldn't know what a married
> woman does or doesn't do.
> Goodnight.

And with that she leaves... Benjamin, left with that
thought...

122A   INT. HOSPITAL ROOM, NEW ORLEANS - DAY, PRESENT   122A

Caroline reading the postcard some sixty odd years
later...

> CAROLINE
> Murmansk. "...I've met
> somebody...and I've
> fallen in love..." Mom?

She hands Daisy the postcard.

> DAISY
> No, that was over sixty years ago.

> CAROLINE
> Did you love him mother?

> DAISY
> What does a girl know about love?

Daisy shuts the cigar box, closing her eyes.

122B   INT. LANDMARK BUILDING, DANCE LOFT, NEW YORK, NIGHT 1941   122B

And we see Daisy, sitting on the dance floor reading the
very same POSTCARD, brokenhearted...

Daisy dances...still just part of the crowd...Now as
Daisy dances...it is filled with pathos and lost
love...and everyone takes notice.

123-124 OMITTED   123-124

Benjamin comes hurrying down the stairs. Elizabeth is
waiting, as she normally is, but this time she is
dressed... Lipstick and hair done... wearing a fur.

> BENJAMIN
> (self-conscious)
> I'm not dressed --

> ELIZABETH ABBOTT
> You look splendid just as you
> are...

She laughs, taking his arm, walking to the dining room as
if going to dinner... They sit at a table... which she
has set for them... Caviar and Vodka...

> ELIZABETH ABBOTT (CONT'D)
> Don't waste any time bothering
> about the wine or the cheese here
> in Murmansk because they really
> are completely ordinary, but the
> caviar and the vodka are sublime
> and plentiful...

She feeds him a spoonful of the caviar...Unaccustomed to
it, he swallows it too quickly...

> ELIZABETH ABBOTT (CONT'D)
> Savor it...and don't eat it all at
> once because that way there's
> nothing left to enjoy...

She takes one herself... He takes his time... They both
do... savoring it...

> ELIZABETH ABBOTT (CONT'D)
> (pouring)
> Now, take a little swallow of
> vodka while it's still in your
> mouth...

Which they do... She laughs... Looking at him...

> ELIZABETH ABBOTT (CONT'D)
> You haven't been with many women
> have you?

(CONTINUED)

                              BENJAMIN
                    Not on Sundays.

                              ELIZABETH ABBOTT
                    And you've never had caviar before
                    have you?

                              BENJAMIN
                    No ma'am.

                              ELIZABETH ABBOTT
                    When I was nineteen, I attempted
                    to become the first woman ever to
                    swim the English Channel...

                              BENJAMIN
                    Really?

126   EXT. THE ENGLISH CHANNEL - DAY, 1911   126

And we see just that....Young Elizabeth, in goggles, her
body covered with grease, swimming with two escort boats
across the English Channel.

                              ELIZABETH ABBOTT'S (V.O.)
                    But the current that day was so
                    strong...that for every stroke I
                    took... I was pushed back two...

And we see just that, Elizabeth fighting the current...

                              ELIZABETH ABBOTT'S (V.O.)
                                (CONT'D)
                    I was in the water for 32 hours...
                    and when I was two miles from
                    Calais...

Elizabeth in sight of the lights of Calais...

                              ELIZABETH ABBOTT'S (V.O.)
                                (CONT'D)
                    ...it started to rain...

And it starts to rain on her... Harder and harder... the
shore is suddenly gone from sight...

                                               (CONTINUED)

                          ELIZABETH ABBOTT'S (V.O.)
                              (CONT'D)
                    When I couldn't go any further, I
                    stopped...I just stopped...

And we see her being taken onto a boat, a blanket wrapped
around her...

127   EXT. CALAIS, BEACH - NIGHT, 1911   127

                          ELIZABETH ABBOTT'S (V.O.)
                    And everybody asked me would I try
                    again...?

                          ELIZABETH ABBOTT
                    Why wouldn't I?

She smiles, a young girl, full of life...

128   INT. DINING ROOM - "WINTER PALACE" - LATE NIGHT, 1941   128

                          ELIZABETH ABBOTT
                    I never did. As a matter of fact,
                    I have never done anything with my
                    life after that...

And it's quiet. She touches his rough hand.

                          ELIZABETH ABBOTT (CONT'D)
                    Your hands are so coarse...

She runs her fingers along his face...

                          ELIZABETH ABBOTT (CONT'D)
                    I can feel the wind on your
                    cheek...

They look at each other. Benjamin kisses her. It
lingers... A clock chimes...she stops herself.

                          ELIZABETH ABBOTT (CONT'D)
                    I'm afraid it's the witching
                    hour...

She quickly gets up... And she's gone. As Benjamin sits
in the empty dining room.

                                                  (CONTINUED)

> BENJAMIN BUTTON'S (V.O.)
> It was the first time a woman had
> ever kissed me. It's something you
> never forget.

129   INT. "WINTER PALACE," RUSSIA - ANOTHER LATE NIGHT, 1941   129

We see Elizabeth nicely dressed, a bottle of champagne in
her hand, anxiously waiting. The elevator descends with
Benjamin in a suit and tie, as handsome as we've seen
him.

130   EXT. MURMANSK, RUSSIA - DEAD OF NIGHT, 1941   130

Their arms in each other's, their breath showing in the
night, they walk out of the hotel through the sleeping
Russian town, their shadows in the moonlight. They pop
the cork and share a drink from the champagne bottle.
They laugh.

> BENJAMIN
> I think you make me feel younger.

And it seems he's about to go on... But Elizabeth,
flattered, takes it metaphorically...

> ELIZABETH ABBOTT
> You make me feel years younger
> too. I wish I was. So many things
> I would change. I would undo all
> of my mistakes.

> BENJAMIN
> What mistakes?

> ELIZABETH ABBOTT
> I kept waiting, you know,
> thinking that I'd do something to
> change my circumstances... Do
> something... It's such an awful
> waste, you never get it back...
> wasted time...

They're quiet. She looks at him.

(CONTINUED)

                              ELIZABETH ABBOTT (CONT'D)
                         (abruptly)
                    If we're going to have an affair,
                    you're never to look at me during
                    the day, and we're always to part
                    before sunrise, and we will never
                    say "I love you..."

He's quiet...

                              ELIZABETH ABBOTT (CONT'D)
                    Those are the rules...

They stand in the cold. He is shivering...

                              ELIZABETH ABBOTT (CONT'D)
                    Are you cold?

                              BENJAMIN
                    I'm freezing.

                              ELIZABETH ABBOTT
                    You are frozen. What an idiot? I
                    stand out here in this fur... How
                    thoughtless of me.

She takes his arm and leads him back...

131   INT. LOBBY, "WINTER PALACE," RUSSIA - LATE NIGHT, 1941   **131**

        Benjamin goes behind the registration desk, taking an
        empty room key off a hook... He crosses to the elevator
        where Elizabeth waits...

132   INT. ELEVATOR, "WINTER PALACE," RUSSIA - LATE NIGHT, 1941 **132**

        They stand in the elevator as it ascends. Anticipating
        what's to come...

133   INT. HALLWAY, "WINTER PALACE," RUSSIA - LATE NIGHT, 1941   **133**

        They move along a dark hallway. He quietly unlocks an
        empty room door... And as he follows her into the room...
        the door closing.

                              BENJAMIN BUTTON'S (V.O.)
                    She was the first woman that ever
                    loved me.

133A   INT. THE HOSPITAL ROOM, NEW ORLEANS - DAY, PRESENT   133A

The wind and rain knocking at the window. Daisy silently
lying in bed.

                CAROLINE
          Do you want me to skip some?

                DAISY
          No. I'm glad he had somebody to
          keep him warm.

Which Caroline takes as her cue to read on...

                CAROLINE
          (after a beat,
           reading)
          "I couldn't wait to see her
          again."

134   INT. "WINTER PALACE," RUSSIA - ANOTHER DAY, 1941   134

Benjamin, in his peacoat, and stocking cap, snow on him,
hurries into the hotel from work... He runs to the
elevator, the doors just closing.

It opens. He goes inside. And Elizabeth's husband is
standing in the elevator.

135   INT. ELEVATOR, "WINTER PALACE," RUSSIA - LATE DAY, 1941   135

They silently ride up, not a word exchanged. The
elevator stops. Elizabeth's husband gets out. As he
quietly walks down the hall...

                BENJAMIN'S (V.O.)
          We saw each other every night...
          we always used the same room...

136   INT. HALL "WINTER PALACE," RUSSIA - NIGHT TO DAWN, 1941   136

We see the key going into the door... Benjamin and
Elizabeth going inside closing the door behind them...
leaving us with the quiet hallway.

                BENJAMIN'S (V.O.)
          But each time seemed new and
          different...

                      (CONTINUED)

And we see them as dawn creeps along the hallway,
Benjamin and Elizabeth, leaving the room, not wanting to
part, passionately kissing, and as they start to go their
separate ways...

                    BENJAMIN
              (whispering)
         Elizabeth...

She turns.

                    BENJAMIN (CONT'D)
              (whispers)
         Goodnight.

And as she laughs to herself and hurries off...

                    BENJAMIN BUTTON'S (V.O.)
         Until one night...

137   INT. "WINTER PALACE," RUSSIA - ANOTHER NIGHT, 1941   137

We see Benjamin coming down the stairs, into the lobby to
meet Elizabeth. And he slows...Elizabeth isn't there. He
looks into the bar...the kitchen....the dining room... He
goes back to the lobby, sitting on a lone sofa, waiting
for her... A mouse runs across the marble floor, stops,
looks at him and runs off... And he sits and waits.

138   INT. LOBBY, "WINTER PALACE," RUSSIA - EARLY MORNING, 1941   138

Snow shrouds the windows. We see Benjamin has fallen
asleep on the sofa... There's the distinctive BELLOW of
Captain Mike's VOICE. Benjamin wakes... He follows the
bellowing to find Captain Mike with the tugboat CREW in
the bar...

                    CAPT. MIKE
         It's a meetin', a policy meetin'
         regarding your future and possibly
         beyond. There's been a change of
         plans lads. As you may or may not
         know the Japs bombed Pearl Harbor
         yesterday. Frank D. Roosevelt's
         asked each of us to do our part!
                    (MORE)

                                          (CONTINUED)

                              CAPT. MIKE (CONT'D)
                    The Chelsea's been commissioned to
                    serve in the United States Navy,
                    to repair, salvage and to
                    rescue... Anybody doesn't want to
                    go to war, now's the time to say
                    so... Once you set foot on that
                    boat, you're in the Navy friend!

And the Cook, Prentiss Mayes...

                              THE COOK
                    Yeah, I been meaning to talk with
                    you Cap'n Mike... My wife's doing
                    poorly. I'd like to maybe see her
                    one more time...

                              CAPT. MIKE
                         (understanding)
                    You're free to make your way home
                    any way you can Mr. Mayes.

And the cook walks off.

                              RICK BRODY
                    If he's leaving who's going to
                    cook?

                              JOHN GRIMM
                         (always dour)
                    Food poisoning is one of the
                    leading causes of death at sea,
                    right after inadequate safety
                    equipment.

                              BENJAMIN
                    I can cook Cap'n. Been doing it
                    all my life.

                              CAPT. MIKE
                    I don't know. You're a little
                    moody for war Benjamin. What the
                    hell. I'll take any mens who wants
                    kick the shit out of the Japs and
                    the Huns.

And with no one dissenting...

                                                    (CONTINUED)

                         CAPT. MIKE (CONT'D)
                 Then that's it! Pack your gear.
                 We're goin to war, gentlemen!

139   INT. BENJAMIN'S ROOM, "WINTER PALACE" LATER, 1941   **139**

Benjamin unlocking the door to his room. An ENVELOPE has
been left under the door, he opens it.

                         BENJAMIN'S (V.O.)
                 She had left a note. She wrote,
                 "it was nice to have met you."
                 That was it.

And as he stands holding the letter in his room at the
small Russian hotel:

140   EXT. TUGBOAT, ATLANTIC OCEAN, SOMEWHERE - NIGHT, 1941   **140**

The men on the tug on a dark grey sea....

                         BENJAMIN BUTTON'S (V.O.)
                 It wasn't the war any of us
                 expected. We would just tow
                 crippled ships... scraps of metal
                 really... If there was a war, we
                 didn't see it...

And what seemed exciting, the idea of war... is
tedious... The "Chelsea" towing a strange hulking shape
on the dark, empty sea...

                         BENJAMIN BUTTON'S (V.O.) (CONT'D)
                 There was a man assigned to us...
                 The Chief Gunner loved the Navy,
                 but most of all, he loved America.

                         THE MAN'S (V.O.)
                 There is no other country in the
                 world...! When YOU spell America,
                 A.M.E.R.I.C.A. You're spelling
                 freedom...!

We see the young Gunnery Mate, no more than nineteen...
sitting at his post on a high caliber machine gun...
ready to kick some enemy ass...

                                               (CONTINUED)

                              BENJAMIN BUTTON'S (V.O.)
                    His name was Dennis Smith and he
                    was a full blooded Cherokee... His
                    family had been Americans for over
                    five hundred years.

                              DENNIS SMITH
                    You have these pacifists. They
                    say they won't fight on
                    conscience. Where would we be if
                    everybody decided to act according
                    to their conscience?

                              CAPT. MIKE
                         (out his Window)
                    Keeps it down, would you chief!

He goes back inside... And as they settle into their
tasks..

141-143 OMITTED   **141-143**

144   INT. CREW QUARTER, TUGBOAT, ATLANTIC OCEAN - NIGHT, 1942   **144**

We see Benjamin awake in his bunk, reading. Pleasant in
the bunk above him...and out of the silence, Pleasant
Curtis for the first time speaks...

                              PLEASANT CURTIS
                    Hey, I've been watching you. You
                    seem trustworthy. If something
                    happens to me... could you see
                    this gets to my wife...?

He hands Benjamin a roll of money...

                              BENJAMIN BUTTON'S (V.O.)
                    He had given me all of his pay...
                    he hadn't spent a dime of it...

                              PLEASANT CURTIS
                    I want my family to know I was
                    thinking about them.

And that said he turns back over...

                                                    (CONTINUED)

                                BENJAMIN BUTTON'S (V.O.)
                        It was the only time I ever heard
                        him say a word to anyone.

And suddenly there's a clanging of a bell:

                                CAPT. MIKE (OVER)
                            (calls)
                        All hands on deck!!!

They bolt from their bunks... Going outside...

145   EXT. TUGBOAT, ATLANTIC OCEAN - NIGHT, 1942   145

Captain Mike stands by the wheelhouse ringing the ship's
bell...The crew emerges on deck...

                                CAPT. MIKE
                        Get your asses up here you lazy
                        bastards!

And as the tug arrives at the scene we see a TRANSPORT
VESSEL, with a gaping hole in its midships sinking
quickly... Fuel oil burning on the water...

The crew stands silently looking at the ocean...

                                BENJAMIN BUTTON'S (V.O.)
                        The war had finally found us.

                                VIC BRODY (O.S.)
                        All stop!

All turn to look towards the stern. The Captain who has
made his way to the 2nd deck turns to Pleasant Curtis.

                                CAPT. MIKE
                        Pleasant, man that light.

He and the others run to the stern of the boat. Benjamin
arrives and looks over the edge into the water.

                                BENJAMIN BUTTON'S (V.O.)
                        A transport carrying 1300 men had
                        been split by a torpedo. We were
                        first to arrive at the scene...

                                                    (CONTINUED)

They see bodies of men, dead men, floating by them... One
and two at first... then three and four... and then more
and more until they are moving through a carpet of
bodies... As they move through the water... their
propeller literally chopping up bodies,

                    BENJAMIN BUTTON
          Cut the engines.

Capt. Mike turns to the wheelhouse and opens the door,
yelling to Grimm.

                    CAPT. MIKE
          All stop! All stop!

Grimm shuts their engines down...

It's then we see the true horror of the men in the
water... in the burning black oil... The transport boat
silently slips into the water, disappearing under the
sea...

146   EXT. TUGBOAT - ATLANTIC OCEAN - NIGHT, 1942   **146**

As the tug moves through the thick black smoke...
Benjamin and the other crewmen watching along the
rails...

                    BENJAMIN BUTTON'S (V.O.)
          We were the only sound...

Except for the lapping of water, there isn't... just the
silence of death... Something else appears, doming onto
the surface like a spectre... the U-BOAT that had reeked
this havoc... looking to see the results...

Pleasant Curtis on the searchlight spots the sub. He
pounds on the window to the wheelhouse. Grimm looks out
and sees what he sees. He yells to the men out on the
stern.

                    JOHN GRIMM
          Fellas!

The men hear his call and all move to the bow. Captain
Mike arrives at the wheelhouse.

                                              (CONTINUED)

                         JOHN GRIMM (CONT'D)
               Sub!

Captain Mike sees the sub...

                         CAPT. MIKE
                    (mad as hell)
               We sure as hell can't outrun them
               fuckers!
                    (and he shouts)
               Battle Stations...!!!

They run to their battle stations...Dennis comes out to
the bow and sees the sub. He rushes back to the ladders
and climbs up to the gun deck.

147   INT. PILOT HOUSE, TUGBOAT, ATLANTIC OCEAN - NIGHT, 1942   **147**

Captain Mike runs into the wheelhouse. John Grimm is
putting on his life vest. Captain hands his pistol to
John Grimm.

Benjamin hands out the life vests. There aren't enough
vests.

                         VIC BRODY
               Is that the last one?

He sacrifices the last vest to one of the Brody twins.

Capt. Mike kills all the running lights then furiously
bears down on the surfaced submarine...

148   EXT. TUGBOAT, ATLANTIC OCEAN - NIGHT, 1942   **148**

A German submariner, on the conning tower, seeing the
Tugboat, turns the .50 caliber machine gun on the
tugboat... Benjamin falls to the deck. The Brody twins
fade back around the starboard side of the boat. John
Grimm fires his pistol at the German. He is hit and falls
dead. Pleasant Curtis is hit by the next round. Dennis
opens up on the U-boat the with the .50 caliber machine
gun. Despite the strafing the tug is relentless... Dennis
is hit with a strafing round and falls to the ground
while still firing.

(CONTINUED)

Another round of gunfire slams into the wheelhouse.
Benjamin sees it and starts up the ladder to the second
deck.

The submarine, seeing it is about to be rammed tries to
dive... but it's too late... the tugboat ramming the
submarine... severing the U-Boat in half. The concussion
of the collision has triggered a torpedo in the sinking
submarine's torpedo shaft, the torpedo exploding,
bursting the submarine, and in the process, blasting away
under the stern of the tugboat... Benjamin hangs onto the
ladder as he swings in the air...One of the Brody twins
is blown to bits. His brother runs to his side. He
manages to get to his feet, the tug listing, beginning to
sink... There's a man's voice...

Benjamin runs into the wheelhouse... And he sees, Captain
Mike riddled with bullets, his body covered with blood...
Benjamin bends to him... Captain Mike trembling rips open
his shirt...

                    CAPT. MIKE
               They shots the hell out my
               paintin'!

His body, his tattoos, like a ripped canvas, is
riddled...

                    CAPT. MIKE (CONT'D)
               Give me your hand.

Captain Mike grabs Benjamin's hand

                    BENJAMIN
               You're going to be alright
               Captain. There's a nice spot in
               heaven waitin' for you. A nice
               spot.

Benjamin sits beside him, his friend Captain Mike, dying.
And a light comes in Captain Mike's eyes... an
understanding.

                    CAPT. MIKE
               You can be mad as a mad dawg at
               the way things wents... You can
               swear, curse the fates...
                         (MORE)
                                                  (CONTINUED)

                              CAPT. MIKE (CONT'D)
                    but when it comes to the end...
                    You have to let go...

And as he holds Benjamin's hand ready to meet his
maker...

149   EXT. ATLANTIC OCEAN - DAY, 1942   149

There are two destroyers and a hospital ship in the
battle zone flow... Planes circling... The water still
speckled with debris, and bodies...

150   EXT. A LIBERTY SHIP, THE NORTH ATLANTIC - DAY, 1942   150

We see Benjamin at the railing of a Liberty Ship... He
watches the sea...

                              BENJAMIN BUTTON'S (V.O.)
                    1328 men died that day... I said
                    my goodbyes to the Cherokee,
                    Dennis Smith, John Grimm who was
                    right, he was going to die
                    there... I sent Pleasant Curtis'
                    wife his money... I said goodbye
                    to the twin, Vic Brody...

                              BENJAMIN BUTTON'S (V.O.) (CONT'D)
                    And to Mike Clark... Captain of
                    the tugboat "Chelsea." I said
                    goodbye to all the other men...
                    who had dreams of their own... All
                    the men who wanted to be insurance
                    salesmen or doctors... or lawyers
                    or Indian chiefs.

A Sailor walks up next to Benjamin carrying one of the
life preservers from The Chelsea. He looks down at the
sinking tug.

                              THE SAILOR
                    This don't get fixed...

Rick Brody looking out a porthole, lost without his twin
brother...

Benjamin reaches for the life preserver. The Sailor
shrugs, giving it to him....

                                                        (CONTINUED)

                            BENJAMIN BUTTON'S
                   Out here, death didn't seem
                   natural.

And suddenly, angrily, he throws the ring into the
water...

Benjamin standing at the rail of the ship... no longer a
boy... Benjamin's quiet. When suddenly a HUMMINGBIRD
comes flying across the water... It circles the wreath,
the way Hummingbirds do... and then flies off...

And as Benjamin stands at the railing, looking at the
sea...

                        BENJAMIN BUTTON'S (V.O.) (CONT'D)
                   In May of 1945.... when I was 26
                   years old... I came home...

151   EXT. THE NOLAN HOUSE, NEW ORLEANS - TWILIGHT, 1945   151

We see Benjamin, suitcase in hand, going up the walk to
the old house. We're struck by the difference... the old
man who had left to see the world has returned a
strikingly handsome man in his fifties. Nothing seems to
have changed. An old woman we don't know is rocking on
the porch. A black girl, just 14... is sweeping...

He goes up the porch, inside....

152   INT. THE NOLAN HOUSE, NEW ORLEANS - TWILIGHT, 1945   152

Some old folks are in the front room... Nobody we know...
He moves by them into the kitchen... the stovetop smoking
and gurgling... He goes into the dining room... Queenie
is busy setting the table... He watches her for a
moment...

                        BENJAMIN
                   (quietly)
              Queenie...

                        QUEENIE
              Yes.

She turns, seeing him... it takes a moment for her to
recognize him. She drops a plate...

                                            (CONTINUED)

                        QUEENIE (CONT'D)
                Oh, sweet Jesus....you're
                home...Lord...You came back. Let
                me look at you.

She runs to embrace him... We see she's aged... the eight
years he's been gone... and the 25 years or so since
we've known her... now in her fifties...

                        THE GIRL'S (V.O.)
                    (asks)
                Who is that momma?

The Girl comes inside... curious...

                        QUEENIE
                Child, it's your brother,
                Benjamin...

                        THE GIRL
                I didn't know he was my brother.

                        QUEENIE
                    (laughs)
                There's a shit load of things you
                don't know child...Get on out
                there and finish sweeping, and
                come in, wash your hands and help
                me with the table. Go on now.

But her interest is in Benjamin....

                        QUEENIE (CONT'D)
                    (studying him)
                Turn around. You look like you
                been born again...younger than the
                springtime... I think that
                preacher that laid the hands on
                you gave you a second life... I
                knew it that moment I saw you --
                you were special... I tell you
                what, my knees is sore 'cause I've
                been on 'em every night asking the
                Lord, I say God, just bring him
                home safely. Remember
                what I told you...?

                                            (CONTINUED)

                              BENJAMIN
                    You never know what's comin' for
                    you.

                              QUEENIE
                    That's right. Sit down...

And they both share a good laugh at her homily... glad to
be together once again.

                              QUEENIE (CONT'D)
                    Well, did you learn anything worth
                    repeating?

                              BENJAMIN
                    I sure saw some things.

She looks in his face...

                              QUEENIE
                    You seen some pain.

He nods.

                              QUEENIE (CONT'D)
                    Some joy too?

                              BENJAMIN
                    Sure. Sure I did.

                              QUEENIE
                    That's what I want to hear. Look
                    at you.

                              BENJAMIN
                    Where's Tizzy?

                              QUEENIE
                    Oh baby, Mr. Weathers died in his
                    sleep one night last April.

                              BENJAMIN
                    Momma, I'm so sorry...

She takes his hand.

                                              (CONTINUED)

> QUEENIE
> Don't you worry about that baby.
> Well, there's only one or two of
> them left now... They all just
> about new... I guess they waitin'
> their turn like everybody else
> huh... I am so glad you're back
> home with me. Now we're gonna have
> to find you a wife and a new job.
> That's right. Come in here and
> help me with this table.

She takes his hand and leads him towards the dining room.

153   OMITTED   153

154   INT. PARLOR, NOLAN HOUSE - NIGHT, LATER, 1945   154

We see Benjamin playing the piano in the parlor, the
particular tune the Woman had taught him... an old woman
sitting nearby, seemingly listening... Queenie, looking
in...

> QUEENIE
> Benjamin. You're wasting your time
> baby...she's stone deaf... Oh and
> you'll be staying in what was Mrs.
> DeSeroux's old room, you're too
> big to be rooming with anybody
> else.

She goes about her business... as Benjamin looks at the
deaf woman.

155   INT. THE PARLOR, NOLAN HOUSE - NIGHT, 1945   155

We see someone helping a patient up the stairs, an old
man asleep on a sofa.

Benjamin listens to the silence of the house...

> BENJAMIN BUTTON'S (V.O.)
> It's a funny thing about coming
> home. Looks the same. Smells the
> same. Feels the same.

Mr. Daws talks to Benjamin. As if he never left.

(CONTINUED)

                              MR. DAWS
                    Did I ever tell you I've been
                    struck by lightning seven times.
                    Once I was sitting in my truck
                    just minding my own business.

And we see just that Mr. Daws sitting in his truck
getting belted by lightning.

                         BENJAMIN BUTTON'S (V.O.)
                    You realize what's changed, is
                    you...

While Benjamin stands looking out the window:

                         BENJAMIN BUTTON'S (V.O.) (CONT'D)
                    Then late one morning, not long
                    after I had been back...

156   INT. THE NOLAN HOUSE - LATE MORNING, 1945   156

We see Benjamin, looking out his bedroom window sees a
TAXI pulling to a stop on the side of the house. A
familiar figure gets out of the cab. The figure of a
young woman, wearing a beret, a dark coat and lace up
boots... He moves to another window to watch as she
strides through the gate... It takes us a moment to
recognize her... the leggy thirteen year old girl is
gone... replaced by a confident woman in her early
twenties... with her red hair and her blue eyes she could
be no one else but DAISY. Benjamin follows her progress,
moving downstairs to the casement window and into the
kitchen, watching her out the windows... Daisy around the
back of the house. The unnamed woman's old dog, smelling
her, comes to greet her... Benjamin moving to the back
door, opening it... Momentarily startled, she doesn't
recognize him.... and asks...

                              DAISY
                    Oh, excuse me... is Queenie
                    here...?

                              BENJAMIN
                    Daisy... it's me, Benjamin.

She hardly can believe her eyes...

                                            (CONTINUED)

                          DAISY
               Benjamin...Oh my God... Of course
               it's you...

They embrace, and there's a moment when the touch is not
just of old friends, but something different... and they
both, in that moment recognize that things will never be
the same... Daisy, over-hugging him... the way young
people do...

                          DAISY (CONT'D)
               Benjamin, how are you? It's been
               such a long time... There's so
               much I want to know... When did
               you come back?

                          BENJAMIN
               Well I got back a few weeks ago...

                          DAISY
               I spoke to Queenie...she said you
               were in the war...somewhere at
               sea... We were so worried about
               you...

                          BENJAMIN
                    (simply)
               I'm okay.

                          BENJAMIN (CONT'D)
               Well look at you -- You are so
               lovely...

                          DAISY
               You stopped writing.

157   INT. HOSPITAL, ROOM, NEW ORLEANS - MORNING, PRESENT   157

                          CAROLINE
                    (reading)
               "When I had left she was a girl...
               and a woman had taken her
               place...She was the most beautiful
               woman I'd ever seen."

                                                        (CONTINUED)

> DAISY
> Beautiful.

> CAROLINE
> "The most beautiful."

158   INT. BACK STAIRS, NOLAN HOUSE - TWILIGHT, 1945   158

Benjamin and Daisy going up the back stairs...

> DAISY
> You remember Grandma Fuller?

> BENJAMIN
> Sure.

> DAISY
> She passed.

> BENJAMIN
> I heard that... I'm sorry...

...They go into her grandmother's room...

159   INT. GRANDMA FULLER'S ROOM - TWILIGHT, 1945   159

Her grandmother's things are in boxes neatly stacked in a
corner, waiting to be taken away...

> DAISY
> I just can't believe we're both
> here...It must be fate...No, what
> do they call it, "Kismet"? Do you
> know about Edgar Cayce? The
> psychic? Well he says everything
> is predetermined...I like to think
> of it as fate.

She brushes some lint off his shoulder... the electricity
of friction... both aware of the closeness... they move
ever so slightly apart...

> BENJAMIN
> I'm not sure how it works, but I'm
> glad it happened...

                                              (CONTINUED)

                              DAISY
                         (nervously)
                    Have you been to Manhattan...?
                    It's right across the river from
                    me... I can see the Empire State
                    Building if I stand on my bed...
                    What about you? Where have you
                    been? Tell me everything. The
                    last time you wrote you said you'd
                    been to Russia? I always wanted
                    to go to Russia... Is it as cold
                    as they say...?

                              BENJAMIN
                    It's twice as cold.

                              DAISY
                         (she looks at him in
                          the mirror)
                    My goodness. We always said you
                    were different. I think you really
                    are.
                         (she turns to him)
                    You wrote you met somebody... did
                    it work out...?

                              BENJAMIN
                    It ran its course. Do you remember
                    this?

He's come upon the BOOK her grandmother had read to them,
Rudyard Kipling's "Just So." He sits on the bed... Daisy
crosses to sit beside him... Daisy looking through the
book... and reading....

                              DAISY
                    "...This is the picture of Old Man
                    Kangaroo at five in the
                    afternoon..."

She looks at him.

                              BENJAMIN
                    Would you like to have dinner?

She smiles at him.

...And we see a taxi door being opened in slow motion...
and Daisy, dressed for the night, glides out... a man
helping her... and we see Benjamin a step behind getting
out of the car... dressed to the nines... hair slicked,
elegant... but nonetheless, a step behind... And we hear
Daisy's voice, from somewhere else...

> DAISY'S (V.O.)
> ...Did I tell you that I danced
> for Ballenchine...He's a famous
> choreographer. He said that I had
> perfect line.

The door to the restaurant held open for Daisy... another
man showing her inside... Benjamin forgotten for the
slightest of moments at the door... going after her.

A crowded New Orleans restaurant. Daisy and Ben enter.
Daisy's coat is taken. The maitre d in slow motion is
showing her to a table... Men's, and even women's, eyes
following her...

They reach a table... A chair in slow motion swept out
for her to sit... another man in slow motion putting a
napkin in her lap...

> DAISY'S (V.O.)
> You know in rehearsal once a
> dancer fell and he put it right
> into the production. Can you
> imagine that in a classical
> ballet? A dancer intentionally
> falling? There's a whole new word
> for dance now, it's called
> abstract...He's not the only one
> though, there's Lincoln Kirstein
> and Lucia Chase and, oh my god,
> Agnes DeMille...She just torn up
> all those conventions...all the
> straight up and down stuff, it's
> not about the formality of the
> dance...it's about what the
> dancer's feeling...

                                        (CONTINUED)

We watch them at the table... Benjamin listening,
appreciating her... her face aglow with the intensity and
the passion of youth... Caviar is brought over...
vodka... We can sense he's telling her what he's learned
from Elizabeth Abbott, how to savor it...He feeds her a
spoonful...They drink the vodka washing it down... she
laughs, delighted...

> BENJAMIN BUTTON'S (V.O.)
> And she told me about this big new
> world... names that didn't mean a
> thing to me...I didn't really hear
> that much of what she was saying.

> DAISY
> ...it's new and it's modern and
> it's American. They understand our
> vigor and our physicality.

And we now hear what she is saying...as she stops
herself...

> DAISY (CONT'D)
> (realizing)
> Oh my god, I've been just talking
> and talking...

> BENJAMIN
> No, I've enjoyed listening...

She takes out a cigarette... He instinctively looks for
matches, a man gets there first, lighting her cigarette
for her... he watches the smoke curl around her...
appreciating her...

> BENJAMIN (CONT'D)
> I didn't know you smoked...

> DAISY
> I'm old enough. I'm old enough
> for a lot of things....

162   EXT. A NEW ORLEANS PARK - NIGHT   162

We see Benjamin and Daisy, their silhouettes walking
through the park...

                                        (CONTINUED)

                          DAISY
               You know in New York we stay up
               all night... watch the sun come up
               over the warehouses... there's
               always something to do...

Which is in stark contrast to Benjamin's life...

They reach a GAZEBO... Not a soul around... Daisy walks
up onto the gazebo.

Daisy, takes off her shoes and her coat...

                          DAISY (CONT'D)
               I have to go back tomorrow...

                          BENJAMIN
               Oh, so soon?

                          DAISY
               I wish I could stay...Dancers...
               don't need costumes or scenery
               anymore.

And showing him what she's been telling him about, she
does a dance for him...

                          DAISY (CONT'D)
               I could imagine dancing completely
               naked...

Daisy, dancing for him... While she dances...

                          DAISY (CONT'D)
               Have you read "D.H. Lawrence," his
               books were banned... The words are
               like making love....

He stands, hands in his pockets appreciating her...as she
dances.

                          DAISY (CONT'D)
               In our company... we have to trust
               each other...Sex...is a part of
               it...You know a lot of the dancers
               are lesbians... There was one
               woman wanted to sleep with me....

                                             (CONTINUED)

She moves closer to him... She comes next to him and she
kisses him... and when he doesn't respond... she tries a
different tact...He's quiet.

                    DAISY (CONT'D)
          Does that upset you?

                    BENJAMIN
          Which part?

                    DAISY
          That somebody wanted to sleep with
          me.

                    BENJAMIN
          You're one desirable woman...I
          would think most of them would
          want to sleep with you...

                    DAISY
          Let's go back to the house...we
          could get a room somewhere... we
          could lay down your jacket...

She takes his hand... There's nothing he'd like more...
but...

                    BENJAMIN
          I don't know Daisy, it's not that
          I wouldn't like to... I think I'd
          just disappoint you...

                    DAISY
          Benjamin, I've been with older
          men.

And despite how available she is, how desirable she is...

                    BENJAMIN
          You're going back to New York
          tomorrow morning. You should be
          with your friends. You're only
          young once...

                    DAISY
          Oh, I'm old enough.

                                        (CONTINUED)

She reaches in for another kiss. Finally he speaks
firmly.

                    BENJAMIN
          Daisy, just not tonight is all.

Daisy, rejected, takes up her shoes... And she starts
off...

                    BENJAMIN (CONT'D)
          We could go hear some music.

Benjamin coming beside her... but they're not really
walking together anymore... and the time for them, this
time, has gone away...

                    BENJAMIN BUTTON'S (V.O.)
          Our lives are defined by
          opportunities. Even the ones we
          miss.

163   INT. HOSPITAL ROOM, NEW ORLEANS - MORNING, PRESENT   **163**

                    DAISY
          He looked so handsome...so
          distinguished...

A Nurse looks in...

                    THE NURSE
          They're sayin' the hurricane's
          going to miss us... blow right on
          by...

                    CAROLINE
          Oh, that's great.

The Nurse goes off down the hall, her voice telling
people the good news...

                    DAISY
               (delirious)
          I'll stay under the blankets with
          my mother. She said nothing would
          happen...Benjamin?

She looks at the book.

                                        (CONTINUED)

                              CAROLINE
                         (after a beat)
                    "Things were becoming
                    different for me..."

164   INT. BENJAMIN'S ROOM, NOLAN HOUSE - NIGHT, 1945   **164**

And we see Benjamin, naked, standing in front of a full
length mirror, looking at himself, studying himself....

                         BENJAMIN BUTTON'S (V.O.)

                    My hair had very little grey and
                    grew like weeds... My sense of
                    smell was keener... my hearing
                    more acute... I could walk further
                    and faster...

He can see outside an ambulance has arrived... to take
away another of the old people...

                         BENJAMIN BUTTON'S (V.O.) (CONT'D)
                    While everybody else was aging...
                    I was getting younger... all
                    alone...

And as he quietly looks at himself... There's a KNOCK on
the door..

                              BENJAMIN
                    Come in.

The door opens and as if to underscore what he's just
said, he sees THOMAS BUTTON in his fifties himself now,
leaning on crutches, his feet bandaged, standing in the
doorway...

                         THOMAS BUTTON
                    Benjamin... Do you remember me?

                              BENJAMIN
                    Sure I do, Mr. Button... What
                    happened to you?

                         THOMAS BUTTON
                    Darn foot got infected...
                    Welcome home, my friend..

The bar and restaurant crowded with men, many with various kinds of handicaps from the war, drinking away their demons... And we see Benjamin and Thomas sitting at a table... thick steaks, baked potatoes, drinks at their elbows...

>   BENJAMIN
>   You're still drinking Sazerac with
>   whiskey.

>   THOMAS BUTTON
>   Creature of habit.

>   BENJAMIN
>   (smiles)
>   Are you still visiting the house
>   on Bourbon street?

>   THOMAS BUTTON
>   (smiles)
>   Not for a long time.

>   THOMAS BUTTON (CONT'D)
>   Interesting times though. We went
>   from making forty thousand to
>   maybe half a million buttons a
>   day... We employed ten times the
>   number of people... We were
>   operating around the clock...

Benjamin looks up and sees a soldier in a wheelchair. The soldier is missing his legs. Thomas turns to look.

>   THOMAS BUTTON (CONT'D)
>   Damn shame. The war's been kind to
>   the button industry.

And he quiets... the sound of the busy restaurant... And after some moments Thomas tells him...

>   THOMAS BUTTON (CONT'D)
>   You know, I'm sick, I don't know
>   how much longer I have...

                                        (CONTINUED)

                  BENJAMIN
         I'm sorry to hear that, Mr.
         Button.

And it seems like he is about to tell Benjamin the entire
truth... but he can't bring himself and instead...

              THOMAS BUTTON
         I don't have any people. I keep to
         myself. I hope you won't mind...
         but whenever possible... I would
         enjoy your company...

              BENJAMIN
         I'll certainly do what I can.

              THOMAS BUTTON
          (after a beat)
         Ben, do you know anything about
         buttons?

166   EXT. BUTTON FACTORY, NEW ORLEANS - NIGHT, 1945   166

An old brick building with a painting on its side of a
woman sewing on a button... "Button's Buttons." A driver
waits outside of a "town car".

167   INT. BUTTON FACTORY, NEW ORLEANS - NIGHT, 1945   167

We see Thomas unlocking a door.

              THOMAS BUTTON
         Button's Buttons has been in our
         family for one hundred and twenty-
         four years.

They come into a corridor.

168   INT. WORK FLOOR, BUTTON FACTORY - NEW ORLEANS - NIGHT   168

They walk through the quiet factory...

Thomas, on his crutches...past the lines of work
benches... Mannequins in uniforms of the armed
services... with their various gold and silver buttons...

                          (CONTINUED)

                         THOMAS BUTTON
               My grandfather was a tailor. He
               had a small shop in Richmond.
               After the Civil War he moved to
               New Orleans where my father had
               the wisdom to make our own
               buttons. So, with his help, the
               tailor shop grew to this... And
               today...
                         (a smile)
               I can't sew a stitch.

Thomas turns on the lights revealing the large button
factory. Benjamin is interested, but the obvious question
is...

                         BENJAMIN
               That's very, very interesting.
               You sure have done well for
               yourself. So, what can I do for
               you, Mr. Button?

And it's as if he has opened a flood gate...

                         THOMAS BUTTON
               Benjamin, you are my son.

And tears run down his anguished face... Benjamin's
still...

                         THOMAS BUTTON (CONT'D)
               I am so sorry I never told you
               before...

Benjamin hasn't moved. The words ring in his ears.

                         THOMAS BUTTON (CONT'D)
               You were born the night the great
               war ended... Your mother died
               giving birth to you... I
               thought... I thought you were a
               monster... I promised your mother
               I'd make sure you were safe... I
               should never have abandoned you...

Benjamin's dead quiet... He looks at this man, his
father...

                                             (CONTINUED)

                              BENJAMIN
                    My mother?

169   INT. THE BUTTON HOUSE, THE GARDEN DISTRICT - NIGHT, 1945   **169**

We see Benjamin and Thomas in a hallway leading to the
kitchen of the large house... The hallway filled with:
photographs of the Button Family. Thomas pointing out
relatives... Family photographs...

                         THOMAS BUTTON
                    The summer house on Lake
                    Pontchartrain. When I was a boy I
                    would love to wake up before
                    anybody else and run down to that
                    lake and watch the day begin. It
                    was as if I was the only one
                    alive.

Benjamin comes to a young Woman's photograph... who could
only be Benjamin's mother. He stops...

                         THOMAS BUTTON (CONT'D)
                    I fell in love with her the first
                    time I saw her.
                         (beat)
                    Your mother's name was Caroline
                    Murphy. She worked in your
                    grandfather's kitchen...She was
                    from Dublin... In 1903 Caroline
                    and all her brothers and sisters
                    came to live here in New Orleans.

He stops at the kitchen door.

                         THOMAS BUTTON (CONT'D)
                    I would find excuses to go down to
                    that kitchen... just so I could
                    look at her...

Benjamin does just that... Looking through the round
window into the empty kitchen... as if she was there
those years ago... as if she was still there...

                                                     (CONTINUED)

                         THOMAS BUTTON (CONT'D)
                    April 25th, 1918, the happiest day
                    of my life, the day I married your
                    mother.

He moves along the hallway... Benjamin looking at the
photographs... his bloodlines... After some moments:

                         BENJAMIN
                    Why didn't you tell me?

Benjamin looks at him.

                         THOMAS BUTTON
                    I plan on leaving everything I
                    have to you...

His "bribe" strikes a nerve.

                         BENJAMIN
                    I have to go.

                         THOMAS BUTTON
                    Where?

                         BENJAMIN
                    Home.

Benjamin turns his back and walks out.

170   INT. QUEENIE'S ROOM - NIGHT, 1946   **170**

Benjamin standing by the door, Queenie sitting up in her
bed...

                         QUEENIE
                       (unforgiving,
                        angrily)
                    What is he thinking?...He think he
                    can just show up, and everything's
                    supposed to be fine and dandy,
                    everybody's just supposed to be
                    friends... He got another thing
                    coming, that's for sure...God be
                    my witness, he got another thing
                    coming.

                                          (CONTINUED)

And with that she turns over, to go back to sleep,
Benjamin turns to leave the room.

                    QUEENIE (CONT'D)
               (not finished)
          That man left us eighteen dollars
          that night you was found. Eighteen
          ratty dollars.

Benjamin turns out the light.

                    BENJAMIN
          Goodnight Momma.

                    QUEENIE
          Goodnight baby.

171   INT. THE NOLAN HOUSE - BACK STAIRS, HALLWAY - NIGHT   171

He climbs the back stairs to his room, as if he's
carrying a terrible burden... as he comes onto the
hallway, Mr. Daws is sitting on his bed with the door
open... Seeing Benjamin...

                    MR. DAWS
          Did I ever tell you I was struck
          by lightning seven times. Once, I
          was walking my dog down the road.

And we see just that, when suddenly he's struck by
lightning. The dog, unharmed, licking his face.

                    MR. DAWS (CONT'D)
          I'm blind in the one eye...I can't
          hardly hear...I get twitches and
          shakes out of nowhere... I always
          lose my line of thought... but you
          know what... God keeps reminding
          me I'm lucky to be alive...
               (a beat, sniffs the
                air)
          Storm's comin'.

Benjamin walks down the hall back to his room.

172   EXT. THOMAS BUTTON'S HOUSE - MIDDLE OF THE NIGHT   172

We see Benjamin knocking on the door of the fashionable
home.

173   INT. THOMAS BUTTON'S HOUSE - MIDDLE OF THE NIGHT   173

Benjamin is let in by the butler into the dark hallway,
quietly walking among the photographs of "his" family. He
goes up the staircase. He goes to his father's room. He
quietly opens the door. The room's dark, his father
asleep. He goes to his father's bed. His father's frail
figure. He wakes him.

                         BENJAMIN
                       (whispers)
               Wake up. Let's get you dressed...

Thomas awakens...seeing Benjamin...

174   OMITTED   174

175   EXT. LAKE PONTCHARTRAIN, LOUISIANA - SUNRISE   175

The endless lake. And we see Mr. Button's chauffeured car
driving along the lake.

176   EXT. THE BUTTON SUMMER HOME, LAKE PONTCHARTRAIN - SUNRISE   176

The car stops in the driveway of an old summer home.
Benjamin helps to put Thomas into his wheelchair.

The house, all closed up. Shuttered. He starts to wheel
his father down the path. The path is too rough...

And he puts his father on his back...His father holding
onto his son, as Benjamin carries him on his back down
to the dock. There's an old wooden deck chair. He helps
his father sit in the chair. And as his father sits for
the last time, watching the lake...

Benjamin sitting at a distance behind him...Both of them
watching the day begin...

And as his father shuts his eyes, sitting in the sun.

                                        (CONTINUED)

> BENJAMIN BUTTON'S (V.O.)
> You can be mad as a mad dog at the
> way things went...You can swear
> and curse the fates, but when it
> comes to the end... You have to
> let go...

177   INT. EMBALMING ROOM, NEW ORLEANS - DAY, 1946   177

A Mortician fills a jar of buttons and puts it on
Thomas's chest as he prepares him for burial.

177A   INT. FUNERAL PARLOR - DAY - 1946   177A

We see Benjamin standing at his father's funeral. His
father lying in the casket. Very few mourners here.

Queenie has come to be with him...to comfort him...

> QUEENIE
> Sure is a beautiful service. He'll
> be buried right next to your
> mother.

> BENJAMIN
> You're my mother.

She takes his arm, always there for him.

> QUEENIE
> My baby.

178   OMITTED   178

179   EXT. NEW YORK CITY — NIGHT, 1947   179

> BENJAMIN BUTTON'S (V.O.)
> Now, I had never seen New York.

We see a cab pull up and Benjamin, in a nice suit,
flowers in hand, daisies, gets out, hurrying into The
Majestic Theater, the marquee telling us "CAROUSEL," is
performing.

180   INT. THE MAJESTIC THEATER, NYC - NIGHT, 1947   180

Benjamin, coming in late, being shown to his seat. And we
see the production of Rodgers and Hammerstein's musical
"Carousel," with Mielziner's seminal stage design, as
choreographed by Agnes De Mille... And we see the dancer
is Daisy...dancing with the man of her dreams, the "bad
boy" carnival barker... while Benjamin watches her.

181   INT. BACKSTAGE, THE MAJESTIC THEATER - NYC - NIGHT, 1947   181

We see Benjamin, flowers in hand, making his way through
a crowded backstage corridor filled with friends and well-
wishers giving cast members congratulations. He comes to
the door... to the attention of a STAGEHAND...

                    BENJAMIN
            Excuse me I'm a friend of
            Daisy's...

The man matter-of-factly opens the door... A dressing
room crowded with dancers changing out of their
Costumes... He calls out...

                    THE MAN
            Daisy has company...

We can hear Daisy's name being said...Benjamin waiting...
He sees Daisy, in a robe, coming through the room....

                    DAISY
            Somebody looking for me?...

...And she sees it's Benjamin. And rather than excited to
see him... She's startled he's there... and not
altogether pleased about him showing up...

                    DAISY (CONT'D)
            Benjamin...

                    BENJAMIN
            Hi.

                    DAISY
            What are you doing here?

                                        (CONTINUED)

And he realizes, as most of us have in one love affair or
another, whatever his expectations may have been, his
fantasy, is not the reality...

                         BENJAMIN
               I thought I'd come visit... spend
               some time with you if I could...

                         DAISY
               I wish you would have called...
               You took me by surprise.

He gives her the flowers, the daisies.

                         BENJAMIN
               You can just throw them out.

                         DAISY
               No. Thank you, they're lovely.

                         BENJAMIN
               I couldn't take my eyes off of
               you... I thought you were
               mesmerizing...

                         DAISY
               Thank you. That's very kind of you
               to say...

There's an awkward moment... and...

                         DAISY (CONT'D)
               I better get changed... a group of
               us are going to a party... would
               you want to come...?

                         BENJAMIN
               Someone told me about a restaurant
               I thought you might enjoy... I
               made a reservation... Just in case
               --

                         DAISY
                    (awkwardly)
               ...all the dancers go out together
               after the show... You're welcome
               to come with us...I'll get changed
               alright?

                                        (CONTINUED)

And she runs back inside the dressing room... Benjamin
left to stand in the hallway....

182   INT. A NEW YORK LOFT - NIGHT, 1947   **182**

A loft elevator opens depositing Benjamin and Daisy along
with a bunch of people into a large loft... crowded with
her friends, dancers and show people, musicians,
predominantly young people, straight and gay, beatniks
before there were beatniks, bohemians... Music playing...
People pressed together, having to shout to talk...

>   DAISY
>   (passing by a woman)
>   She choreographs for ballet Russ.
>   She's divine.

She pauses at another woman

>   DAISY (CONT'D)
>   You were breathtaking.

She is startled as a young man, DAVID, suddenly grabs
her, Daisy obviously involved with him... but embarrassed
by the intimacy in front of Benjamin and not wanting to
hurt his feelings... she pulls awkwardly away from him...

>   DAISY (CONT'D)
>   This is David... He dances with
>   the company... This is Benjamin.
>   I've told you about him.

Daisy, wanting to escape.

>   DAVID
>   Oh yeah, how you doing?

>   DAISY
>   I'll go get you a drink. - -

...she goes into the kitchen...

>   DAVID
>   So you were a friend of her
>   grandmother's or something like
>   that...?

>   (CONTINUED)

                              BENJAMIN
                    Something like that.

                              DAVID
                    Excuse me.

And Daisy comes back out with a drink for him... and one
of her own... But before she can give him his drink, a
dancer starts to dance with her... but not with her...
the way dancers do... and many of the dancers are dancing
just because they feel like it... David, comes to dance
with Daisy... Benjamin standing watching Daisy dancing
with him... as only dancers can... in complete control of
their bodies and yet totally uninhibited... Benjamin sees
David kiss her... and his jealousy getting the best of
him, he turns and leaves...

183   OMITTED   **183**

184   EXT. NEW YORK STREET - NIGHT, 1947   **184**

Benjamin on his way out of the apartment coming along the
street. Daisy running after him...

                              DAISY
                    Hey! Now I had no idea you were
                    coming. Lord Benjamin, what did
                    you expect? What, did you want me
                    to just drop everything... this is
                    my life...

And we see DAVID and a group of her dancer friends have
come outside down the way into the street...A cab pulls
up and they start piling in.

                              DAVID
                         (to Daisy)
                    Hey, are we going downtown?

                              DAISY
                         (conflicted, to
                          Benjamin)
                    Come on, you'll have a good time.
                    There's lots of musicians,
                    interesting people....

                                                    (CONTINUED)

                         BENJAMIN
          You don't have to do that. This is
          my fault. I should've called. I
          thought I was gonna come in here
          and sweep you off your feet or
          something.

                         DAVID
          Daisy, come on.

                         DAISY
          Be right there.

She's torn... between her life and some other life...
Benjamin, recognizing her conflict...

                         BENJAMIN
          He seems nice. Do you love him?

185   OMITTED   185

186   EXT. THE MANHATTAN STREET - NIGHT, 1947   186

                         DAISY
          I think so.

                         BENJAMIN
                    (understanding)
          I'm happy for you...maybe I'll see
          you at home...

Daisy starts backing towards the cab.

                         DAISY
          Okay.

Benjamin watches her.

                         BENJAMIN
                    (yelling after her)
          I enjoyed the show.

He turns to go... she does what we all do in these
moments, what feels good at the time... She runs to be
with her friends... She gets into a taxi... And another
chance for them is missed... The street's quiet. And
hands in his pockets, a middle-aged man going on 29... he
walks off into the night...

INT. HOSPITAL ROOM, NEW ORLEANS - MORNING, PRESENT

                    DAISY
               (remembers)
          He came to tell me his father had
          died.

                    CAROLINE
          You couldn't have known.

                    DAISY
          I was 23...I just didn't care...

                    CAROLINE
          What did you do next?

                    DAISY
          ...some photographs I
          think...in front of my grey bag.

Caroline goes to the suitcases... she comes back with a
manila envelope... Daisy dumps them out...and we see
they're photographs of Daisy dancing at the height of her
abilities...

                    DAISY (CONT'D)
          I was as good a dancer as I was
          ever going to be. For five
          years... I danced everywhere... In
          London, Vienna, Prague...

She watches Caroline looking at the photos.

                    CAROLINE
          I've never seen these. Mom, you
          never talked about your dancing.

                    DAISY
          Well, I was the only American to
          be invited to dance with the
          Bolshoi... It was glorious...

EXT. MOSCOW STREET - NIGHT, 1952

And we see Daisy, five years older, her arm inside a tall
young blond Russian dancer's, ANITOLY, crossing a snowy
street in Moscow...

                                        (CONTINUED)

                              DAISY (V.O.)
                   But Benjamin was never far from my
                   thoughts...

188A   INT. BENJAMIN'S ROOM, NOLAN HOUSE - NIGHT, 1952   188A

        We see Benjamin in bed, turning off the light...

189   INT. MOSCOW APARTMENT - NIGHT, 1952   189

        Daisy in bed, the young Russian dancer Anitoly lying
        beside her, asleep... Daisy, looking off...

                              DAISY'S (V.O.)
                   And I'd find myself saying...

                              DAISY
                   Goodnight, Benjamin...

190   INT. BENJAMIN'S ROOM, NOLAN HOUSE - NIGHT 1952   190

        Benjamin lying in bed.

                              BENJAMIN
                        (a beat, saying)
                   Goodnight, Daisy.

        And as they both lie in their beds... thinking of the
        other...

191   INT. THE HOSPITAL ROOM - DAY, THE PRESENT   191

                              DAISY
                   He said that?

                              CAROLINE
                   "Life wasn't all that complicated.
                   If you want you might say I was
                   looking for something."

191A   INT. GARAGE - NOLAN HOUSE - DAY   191A

        Benjamin uncovers Tizzy's old motorcycle.

192   EXT. THE BAYOU, LOUISIANA - DAY   192

        We see Benjamin on Tizzy's old motorcycle riding along
        the backroads of the endless swamps known as the bayou.

193   EXT. THE NOLAN HOUSE - AN EARLY EVENING, 1954   193

        Benjamin in work clothes on a ladder, painting some old
        window shutters... Queenie comes out... to tell him...

                         QUEENIE
                    Benjamin, Mrs. La Tourneau just
                    passed.

        Benjamin nods.

        A Messenger on a bicycle rides up...Benjamin comes down
        the ladder.

                    A WESTERN UNION MESSENGER
                    Mr. Benjamin Button...

        Queenie points to Benjamin on her way back into the
        house.

                         BENJAMIN
                    That would be me....

        The Messenger gives him the telegram and getting his tip,
        rides off, Benjamin opens the telegram.

194   EXT. A STREET IN PARIS, FRANCE - DAY, 1954   194

        We see Benjamin, getting out of a cab in Paris... in
        front of an old HOSPITAL... runs up the stairs...

195   INT. A HOSPITAL, PARIS, FRANCE - DAY, 1954   195

        Benjamin crosses an old tile floor to a reception desk...
        He asks for Daisy...

                         BENJAMIN
                    Bonjour.

                         THE WOMAN
                    Oui Monsieur.

                                              (CONTINUED)

                          BENJAMIN
              Miss Daisy Fuller

                          WOMAN
              Just a minute... please have a
              seat...

The woman calls on the phone.

                          WOMAN (CONT'D)
              Avez vous le numero du lit de
              Mademoiselle Fuller.

Benjamin sits in the waiting room.

                          BENJAMIN BUTTON'S (V.O.)
              Sometimes we are on a collision
              course and we just don't know
              it... Whether it's by accident or
              by design, there's not a thing we
              can do about it... A woman in
              Paris was on her way to go
              shopping...

And we will see just what he is describing...

                          BENJAMIN BUTTON'S (V.O.) (CONT'D)
              But she had forgotten her coat...
              and went back to get it... And
              when she had gotten her coat the
              phone had rung... and so she had
              stopped to answer it... and talked
              for a couple of minutes...

And we see just that,..

                          BENJAMIN BUTTON'S (V.O.) (CONT'D)
              And while the woman was on the
              phone; Daisy was rehearsing for a
              performance at the Paris Opera
              House...

And we See Daisy, in her late twenties now, at the peak
of her abilities, rehearsing for that evening's
performance...

                                              (CONTINUED)

> BENJAMIN BUTTON'S (V.O.) (CONT'D)
> And while she was rehearsing...
> the woman, off the phone now...
> had gone outside... to get a
> taxi...

The Woman standing in the street, hand raised, looking
for a taxi. A Cab comes to a stop....she moves to get
it... but somebody gets there first...the cab driving
off... and as she waits for the next cab...

> BENJAMIN BUTTON'S (V.O.) (CONT'D)
> Now a taxi driver... had dropped
> off a fare earlier... and had
> stopped to get a cup of coffee...

A Taxi parked... Its Driver finishing a cup of coffee...

> BENJAMIN BUTTON'S (V.O.) (CONT'D)
> And all the while Daisy was
> rehearsing...

And we see just that...

> BENJAMIN BUTTON'S (V.O.) (CONT'D)
> And this cab driver who had
> dropped off the earlier fare, and
> stopped to get the cup of
> coffee... picked up the lady, who
> was going shopping... who had
> missed getting the earlier cab...

We see the Woman riding in the taxi of the now familiar
cab driver... the taxi, has to stop for a man running
across the Street.

> BENJAMIN BUTTON'S (V.O.) (CONT'D)
> The taxi had to stop for a man
> crossing the street who had left
> for work five minutes later than
> he normally did... because he
> forgot to set his alarm...

We see the man sleeping... The silent alarm clock on the
bedstand...

                                                    (CONTINUED)

> BENJAMIN BUTTON'S (V.O.) (CONT'D)
> ...While that man, late for work,
> was crossing the street... Daisy
> had finished rehearsing and was
> taking a shower.

And we see...Daisy showering,..

> BENJAMIN BUTTON'S (V.O.) (CONT'D)
> ...While Daisy was showering, the
> taxi was waiting outside a
> Boutique for the woman to pick up
> a package... which hadn't been
> wrapped yet because the girl who
> was supposed to wrap it... had
> broken up with her boyfriend the
> night before and forgot...

The Girl standing outside the back of the Boutique,
crying, brokenhearted...

> BENJAMIN BUTTON'S (V.O.) (CONT'D)
> When the package was wrapped...
> The woman was back in the cab...
> it was blocked by a delivery
> truck...

We see the Taxi blocked by a delivery truck... the cab
driver honking...

> BENJAMIN BUTTON'S (V.O.) (CONT'D)
> All the while Daisy was getting
> dressed...

Daisy getting dressed...

> BENJAMIN BUTTON'S (V.O.) (CONT'D)
> The Delivery truck pulled away and
> the taxi was able to move...

The taxi, moving off...

> BENJAMIN BUTTON'S (V.O,) (CONT'D)
> While Daisy, the last to be
> dressed, waited for one of her
> friends who had broken a
> shoelace...

We see her friend breaking her shoelace while tying it...

> BENJAMIN BUTTON'S (V.O.)
> While the taxi was stopped,
> waiting for a traffic light...

We see just that, the taxi stopped for a light.

> BENJAMIN BUTTON'S (V.O.)
> Daisy and her friend came out the
> back of the theater...

Daisy and her friend, carrying their dance bags, coming
out of the theater... They start to cross the street...
Daisy, showing her friend a tight pirouette, when we see
the Taxi, rounding the corner...

> BENJAMIN BUTTON'S (V.O.) (CONT'D)
> And if only one thing had happened
> differently... if that shoelace
> hadn't broken...

And we see the shoelace not breaking...

> BENJAMIN BUTTON'S (V.O.) (CONT'D)
> ...Or that delivery truck had
> moved moments earlier...

The delivery truck leaving earlier...

> BENJAMIN BUTTON'S (V.O.) (CONT'D)
> ...Or that package had been
> wrapped and ready... because the
> girl hadn't broken up with her
> boyfriend...

The girl and boy happily kissing...

> BENJAMIN BUTTON'S (V.O.) (CONT'D)
> ...Or that man had set his alarm
> and got up five minutes earlier.

The man's alarm going off, waking him up...

> BENJAMIN BUTTON'S (V.O.) (CONT'D)
> ...Or that taxi driver hadn't
> stopped for a cup of coffee...

(CONTINUED)

The Driver passing by the cafe...

>   BENJAMIN BUTTON'S (V.O.) (CONT'D)
>   ...Or that woman had remembered
>   her coat...

The woman remembering to take her coat...

>   BENJAMIN BUTTON'S (V.O.) (CONT'D)
>   ...And had gotten into an earlier
>   cab...

The woman getting into the other cab... she beats
somebody for...

>   BENJAMIN BUTTON'S (V.O.) (CONT'D)
>   Daisy and her friend would have
>   crossed the street...

Daisy and her friend crossing the street... Daisy,
showing her friend her dance move, doing a pirouette...

>   BENJAMIN BUTTON'S (V.O.) (CONT'D)
>   ...and the taxi would have driven
>   by...

And we see the taxi turning the corner, driving safely by
them... and becoming a ghost... of what might have
been...

Benjamin waiting. The receptionist answers the phone.

>   WOMAN
>   Recepcion. Oui. Monsieur.

Benjamin stands. She hands him a piece of paper.

Benjamin checks the paper and the number on the door. He
enters the ward.

>   BENJAMIN BUTTON'S (V.O.)
>
>   But life being what it is... a
>   series of intersecting lives and
>   incidents... Out of anyone's
>   control... that taxi did not go
>   by... and that driver was
>   momentarily distracted...

                                            (CONTINUED)

The Driver wipes cigarette ash from his shirt front
momentarily looking down...

Daisy and her friend crossing the Street, Daisy doing the
Pirouette...

And we see just that... Daisy being slammed into by the
taxi... thrown a distance... lying crumpled in the
Street...

> BENJAMIN BUTTON'S (V.O.) (CONT'D)
> ...and that taxi hit Daisy...

196   INT. A HOSPITAL ROOM, PARIS, FRANCE - DAY, 1954   196

We see Benjamin coming into the hospital room in
France...

> BENJAMIN BUTTON'S (V.O.)
> And her leg was crushed...

Daisy, fully immobilized, lying in a hospital bed...She's
still, her eyes closed. Sensing him, she stirs. And then
she sees him.

> BENJAMIN
> Daisy...

> DAISY
> Who told you?

> BENJAMIN
> Your friend wired me.

> DAISY
> ....very kind of you... to come
> all this way, to see that I was
> alright.

> BENJAMIN
> You would do the same for me...

And her first reaction, to how young he is...

> DAISY
> My God, look at you. You're
> perfect....

> (CONTINUED)

Which she isn't... She's quiet, and she suddenly says:

>   DAISY (CONT'D)
>   I wish you hadn't of come.

He's dead still.

>   DAISY (CONT'D)
>   I didn't want you to see me like
>   this...

She tries to pull herself up... Before he can say
anything... A Nurse comes in saying something in
French... Benjamin waits...

>   BENJAMIN BUTTON'S (V.O.)
>   Her leg had been broken in five
>   places.... and with therapy, and
>   time, she might walk again...but
>   she would never dance...

Benjamin sits back down. Daisy turns her face away from
him.

>   BENJAMIN
>   I'm gonna take you home with me. I
>   want to look after you.

She suddenly turns...

>   DAISY
>   I'm not going back to New Orleans.

>   BENJAMIN
>   Then I'll stay here in Paris...

>   DAISY
>   Benjamin...! Don't you understand?
>   I don't want your help. I know I'm
>   feeling sorry for myself but I
>   don't want to be with you... I
>   tried to tell you that in New
>   York... You don't listen...

>   BENJAMIN
>   You might change your mind.

                                        (CONTINUED)

                          DAISY
              We're not little children anymore
              Benjamin. Just stay out of my
              life!

And she turns away from him again...It's dead still...
and we look at her...eyes closed... And after some
moments she turns back to look at Benjamin... And there
are just the curtains billowing in the breeze... Benjamin
is gone...

197   INT. THE HOSPITAL, NEW ORLEANS - DAY, PRESENT   197

                          DAISY
              I was awfully cruel. He didn't
              understand. I couldn't have him
              see me like that.

                        CAROLINE
              "I didn't leave right away. I
              stayed in Paris for awhile to look
              out for her..."

197A   EXT. PARIS - DAY   197A

Benjamin walking the streets of Paris.

197B   INT. HOSPITAL ROOM, NEW ORLEANS - DAY, PRESENT   197B

                          DAISY
              I never knew that.

197C   EXT. PARIS - DAY   197C

Benjamin in Paris, looking up at Daisy's window.

197D   INT. THE HOSPITAL ROOM, NEW ORLEANS - DAY, PRESENT   197D

Daisy in bed...she winces with pain...her breathing
becoming ragged...

                          DAISY
              Darling, could you get the nurse?

She goes into the hall...Daisy left to deal with the
remnants of her mortality...

                                              (CONTINUED)

                          DAISY (CONT'D)
                I taught myself to walk again. I
                took the train to Lourdes.

The nurse coming into the room...Caroline behind
her...times her pulse.

                          NURSE
                Let's take a look. That's normal.
                Pulse rate is slowing. She is
                gonna struggle to breathe. Will
                you be alright?

                          CAROLINE
                Yeah.

She leaves. Daisy looks at Caroline as if to say, "What
happened to him...?" Caroline grabs the diary.

                          CAROLINE (CONT'D)
                Alright, he says "I went back
                home," and then there's a lot of
                pages torn out..."I listened to
                the sound of the house..."

Caroline stands and paces.

                          CAROLINE (CONT'D)
                I think I read that already...He
                spilt something on it so it's hard
                to read. Something about
                "sailing". Does that make sense?

198   OMITTED   198

199   EXT. LAKE PONTCHARTRAIN, LOUISIANA - ANOTHER DAY, 1960   199

We see a SAILBOAT out on the lake...

                          BENJAMIN BUTTON'S (V.O.)
                I learned to sail on an old boat
                of my father's from the Lake
                House...

And we see Benjamin, the wind in his hair, sailing an old
sailboat... And the change in his appearance is
startling... His hair is without a trace of gray...

                                              (CONTINUED)

His face with barely a wrinkle, chiseled...He is a
healthy man in his 40s now...

> BENJAMIN BUTTON'S (V.O.) (CONT'D)
> I can't lie, I did enjoy the
> company of a woman or two...

200   EXT. A NEW ORLEANS RESTAURANT - NIGHT   200

Benjamin and a Woman standing on the sidewalk outside a
restaurant, in the middle of an ardent kiss... As a taxi
pulls up...

200A   EXT. A NEW ORLEANS HOUSE - DAYBREAK   200A

Benjamin at the door kissing another Woman
goodbye...going home

200B   INT. BENJAMIN'S ROOM, NOLAN HOUSE - EARLY ANOTHER   200B
        MORNING, 1960

Benjamin's door opening...Another Woman, disheveled,
coming out of his room...

> BENJAMIN BUTTON'S (V.O.)
> ...Or maybe three...

We see a cluster of old people, ready for the day,
looking at her coming out...the woman making her way
awkwardly down the stairs...Benjamin sitting on his bed
looks to the window. He crosses and looks out. If we
didn't know any better he seems to be waiting for someone
to come home.

201   EXT. THE STREET, BY NOLAN HOUSE - END OF THE DAY, 1962 201

We see Benjamin riding the old motorcycle along the
street on his way home...

202   EXT. THE NOLAN HOUSE - END OF THE DAY, 1962   202

He comes to the gate, opening it, coming into the yard,
shutting the gate behind him. One of the helpers rakes
leaves in the back yard.

> BENJAMIN
> I don't know why you bother Sam,
> they're just gonna be there again
> tomorrow.

                                            (CONTINUED)

Queenie, for some reason, is standing on the back porch
...an apron in her hands... She nods to Benjamin... she
seems to be watching Benjamin, as he walks around the
house -- to the back door.

                        BENJAMIN (CONT'D)
        Momma.

He walks up the back steps, and starts to open the
kitchen door, when he senses behind him... DAISY, now 37,
but still with her unmistakable blue eyes, is standing
there...

                        BENJAMIN BUTTON'S (V.O.)
        And in the spring of 1962 she came
        back.

They look at each other in silence...and they simply
smile, so glad to see each other after all the missing
years... They embrace...for some time... As people who
haven't seen each other, and have thought about each
other... for a very long time... And it just is...no big
symphonies, no endless skies...just, two people at a
kitchen door in the middle of their lives... and the
simplicity, just that, is what makes it real and breaks
your heart.

203 INT. THE KITCHEN, NOLAN HOUSE - THAT NIGHT, 1962   **203**

A radio plays... they sit at the dining table, the
conversation muted... They don't know really where to
begin, where did they leave off...so they don't begin
until they can....

                        DAISY
        Do you want to know where I've
        been?

                        BENJAMIN
        No.

Queenie comes in and sets a piece of pie in front of
Daisy.

                                                (CONTINUED)

                        QUEENIE
                    (pure Queenie)
            How come you didn't write or
            nothin'? Just disappearing like
            that?

                        DAISY
            It was something I needed to do
            for myself.

                        QUEENIE
            Well, I never took you to be the
            selfish type. I sure hope I'm not
            wrong. I'm usually not wrong about
            people.

And Queenie leaves the room...

                        BENJAMIN
            Goodnight Momma.

                        QUEENIE
            Goodnight baby. Y'all have fun.

Benjamin slightly smiles. They look at each other.

                        DAISY
            You haven't said two words.

                        BENJAMIN
            I don't want to ruin it...

And they sit quietly in the kitchen, looking at each
other, silently...

204   INT. BACK STAIRWAY - NOLAN HOUSE - THAT NIGHT, 1962   204

Benjamin carries her bags upstairs. They reach the third
floor.

205   INT. HALLWAY, NOLAN HOUSE - 3RD FLOOR - THAT NIGHT, 1962   205

All the years seem to surround them. They walk along the
corridor to Daisy's room. What was her grandmother's
room. She opens the door.

He sets her bags down. Queenie despite her reservations
has left some clean towels on the bed for her... There's
an inept quiet. The two of them with nothing left to
say... And they listen to the quiet... The house with its
symphony of night noises...Daisy turns and closes the
door.

> DAISY
> Sleep with me.

> BENJAMIN
> Absolutely.

He walks to her. They look at each other. And they kiss,
A kiss that has waited for thirty years. A kiss that has
waited a lifetime. And yes, there is passion... and
need... but most particularly, the awkwardness of people
discovering each other for the first time... While he
gently, tenderly, kisses her, undresses her..

Daisy loosens her hair. Benjamin unzips her dress. Daisy
begins to remove her stockings. Benjamin sees her scarred
knee and runs his hand over it. She puts her hand on his
and turns to face him. They lay back on the bed, kissing,
caressing...

They kiss more and more passionately...as they make love
in the old bedroom...

> BENJAMIN BUTTON'S (V.O.)
> I asked her to come away with
> me...

What follows feels like a HOME MOVIE...without any sound.

207   EXT. THE FLORIDA GULF COAST - ANOTHER DAY, 1963   207

And we see the small sailboat out on the gulf coast...

> BENJAMIN BUTTON'S (V.O.)
> We sailed into the Gulf... along
> the Florida Keys...

208   EXT. THE FLORIDA COAST, A COVE - DAY, 1963   208

Daisy and Benjamin on the sailboat at a cove on the
Florida coast. They watch a ROCKET, soaring into space
from Cape Canaveral. As they watch it roar overhead,
Benjamin marvels at its power...leaving its trail across
the sky...Daisy, not so much interested, taking his arm,
taking him back down below...

209   EXT. THE CARIBBEAN, ANOTHER COVE - DAY, 1963   209

Daisy washing her hair off the side of the boat.

210   EXT. THE CARIBBEAN, ANOTHER COVE - DAY   210

The boat anchored. Benjamin and Daisy sitting on the
beach having a picnic.

211   EXT. THE CARIBBEAN, ANOTHER COVE - DAY, 1963   211

The boat in still another cove. Daisy and Benjamin in
the water. Just their eyes above the dark water looking
only at each other.

212   EXT. THE BOAT - CARIBBEAN - NIGHT, 1963   212

Under millions of stars. Benjamin and Daisy making love
on a blanket on the deck...

Diving off the boat into the water.

213   EXT. THE CARIBBEAN, AN ISLAND BEACH - DAY, 1963   213

Benjamin and Daisy making love on a secluded beach.

                 DAISY'S (V.O.)
I'm so glad we didn't find one
another when I was 26.

                 BENJAMIN'S (V.O.)
Why?

                 DAISY'S (V.O.)
I was so young and you were so
old. It happened when it was
supposed to happen.

214   EXT. THE CARIBBEAN - ANOTHER DAY, 1963   214

The boat tossing out on the water...threatening clouds on
the horizon...

215   INT. A CARIBBEAN HOTEL, BAR - DAY, 1963   215

A small Caribbean hotel. We see Benjamin and Daisy
sitting at a table drinking, talking in a nearly empty
bar... wind and rain lashing the hotel... waiting out a
tropical storm...

>   BENJAMIN'S (V.O.)
>   I'm going to enjoy each and every
>   moment I have with you...

And the wind changes direction, the rain coming in
through the open windows of the bar, getting them wet...
people run for cover...

>   DAISY
>   Bet I can stay out here longer
>   than you can.

>   BENJAMIN
>   I bet you can't.

And as they both sit doggedly in the rain...

216   INT. HOTEL ROOM, THE CARIBBEAN HOTEL - NIGHT, 1963   216

A white hotel room... The storm shutters closed... The
wind and the rain banging at the shutters... Daisy and
Benjamin lying together on a bed out of the storm... She
touches his face as if for the first time...

>   DAISY
>   You barely have a line, or a
>   crease... Every day I have more
>   wrinkles...It's not fair.

>   BENJAMIN
>   I love your wrinkles, both of
>   them.

>   DAISY
>   What's it like growing
>   younger?

                                        (CONTINUED)

                         BENJAMIN
               I can't really say... I'm always
               looking out my own eyes...

They're quiet, just the sound of the rain and the
chattering shutters... She lays closer to him...
warmly... She smiles...

                         DAISY
               Will you still love me when I when
               my skin grows old and saggy...

Benjamin laughs. And his answer is...

                         BENJAMIN
               Will you still love me when I have
               acne, when I wet the bed, when I'm
               afraid of what's under the stairs.

Daisy senses something is wrong.

                         DAISY
               What?

                         BENJAMIN
               Nothing.

He shakes his head. Daisy rolls over to look at him.

                         DAISY
               What are you thinking?

                         BENJAMIN
               I was thinking how nothing lasts
               and what a shame that is...

                         DAISY
               Some things last...

Benjamin moves closer to Daisy.

                         BENJAMIN
               Goodnight Daisy.

                         DAISY
               Goodnight Benjamin.

They kiss...

217   OMITTED   217

218   INT. HOSPITAL ROOM, NEW ORLEANS - DAY, THE PRESENT   218

       And Caroline's stopped reading...

                         CAROLINE
                Mom?

                         DAISY
                Mmm hmmm.

                         CAROLINE
                    (after a beat)
                When did you meet Dad?

                         DAISY
                Some time after that...

                         CAROLINE
                Did you ever tell him about this
                Benjamin?

                         DAISY
                He knew enough darling.

219   OMITTED   219

220   EXT. THE NOLAN HOUSE, NEW ORLEANS - ANOTHER DAY, 1963   220

       We see Daisy and Benjamin, with their few belongings,
       returning home... They go up the walkway... Benjamin
       trots up the steps, opens the screen door and goes
       inside...

221   INT. THE NOLAN HOUSE, NEW ORLEANS - ANOTHER DAY, 1963   221

       Benjamin comes inside... Daisy's just behind him... The
       front room is empty... The house still...

       He looks into the parlor... The piano... He goes down a
       hallway into the kitchen...

                         BENJAMIN
                Momma? Queenie...?

                                              (CONTINUED)

Nobody... He goes down the hall looking in Queenie's
small room under the stairs... Nobody's there... He moves
back into the front room... calling...

                    THE OLD WOMAN
              Hello?

When finally an old Woman, who's been sleeping, comes to
the top of the stairs...

                    BENJAMIN
              Hi Mrs. Carter, it's Benjamin, ...
              Where is everybody?

                    THE OLD WOMAN
              Oh Benjamin...Queenie died. I'm so
              sorry.

222   INT. A BLACK BAPTIST CHURCH, NEW ORLEANS - DAY, 1963   222

The church is crowded... And we see Benjamin and Daisy,
in the front row ... They are the only white people
there. People clap as the choir sings "I'll Fly Away."

                    BENJAMIN BUTTON'S (V.O.)
              We buried her beside her beloved
              Mr. Weathers...

223   OMITTED   223

224   EXT. THE BUTTON HOUSE, GARDEN DISTRICT - DAY, 1963   224

The old house, in a now decaying New Orleans
neighborhood... but despite the faltering area, the house
retains a dignity of its own...

                    BENJAMIN BUTTON'S (V.O.)
              And so we might have memories of
              our own we sold my Father's house
              on Esplanade...

225   INT. THE BUTTON HOUSE - ANOTHER DAY, 1963   225

Benjamin walks around the corner to see the Real Estate
Agent shaking the hand of an OLDER MAN.... quite a bit
older...

His young pregnant wife comes to the door...

                                              (CONTINUED)

And he sees his wife... pleased to see her... hugging
her... tenderly kissing her... and their age difference
readily obvious... Benjamin acutely aware of it...

                    THE WOMAN
          It's a wonderful old place,
          darling... I think we are going to
          be so happy here...

They go into the hallway lined with the family
photographs... She's taken by them...

                    THE WOMAN (CONT'D)
          Oh, what a long family history you
          have...

                    BENJAMIN
          They come with the house...

                    BENJAMIN BUTTON'S (V.O.)
          And we bought ourselves a duplex.

226   EXT. A SUBURBAN TOWNHOUSE, NEW ORLEANS - DAY, 1963   226

Benjamin and Daisy walk up the steps to a suburban New
Orleans townhouse.

227   INT. HOSPITAL ROOM, NEW ORLEANS - DAY, PRESENT   227

                    DAISY
               (murmurs)
          I loved that house... it smelled
          like firewood...
               (in bliss)
          Don't...Don't stop darlin'...

She closes her eyes...

                    CAROLINE'S (V.O.)
          "It was one of the happiest times
          of my life..."

                    BENJAMIN BUTTON'S (V.O.)
          We didn't have a stick of
          furniture. We lived right on the
          floor.

228   INT. THE SUBURBAN TOWNHOUSE, NEW ORLEANS - DAY, 1963   228

Benjamin and Daisy move in to the apartment; boxes, the
mattress.

                    BENJAMIN BUTTON'S (V.O.)
                We ate when we felt like it.
                Stayed up all night when we
                wanted.

Benjamin makes a fire in the fireplace and the place
fills with smoke.

229   INT. BEDROOM, SUBURBAN TOWNHOUSE, NEW ORLEANS DAY, 1963   229

We see Benjamin and Daisy sleeping on a mattress on the
floor in the living room...

                    BENJAMIN BUTTON'S (V.O.)
                We vowed never to fall into a
                routine, to go to bed or wake up
                at the same time. It was life on a
                mattress...

And we see just that, a short film of two people who
can't get enough of each other living on a mattress...
Daisy and Benjamin at various times, while they are
fixing up their apartment. They either sleep, or talk,
or watch TV, or make love, ON THE MATTRESS ON THE
FLOOR...

                    BENJAMIN BUTTON'S (V.O.) (CONT'D)
                Our neighbor, Mrs. Van Dam was a
                physical therapist...

230   INT. PORCH, SUBURBAN TOWNHOUSE, NEW ORLEANS - DAY, 1963   230

We see Daisy in the back yard, exercising her leg under
the supervision of an older woman... MRS. VAN DAM...

                    BENJAMIN BUTTON'S (V.O.)
                We lived four blocks from a public
                pool...

INT. A PUBLIC SWIMMING POOL, YWCA - DAY, 1963

We see Daisy in a bathing suit, resting from swimming,
holding on to the side of the pool, watching a young,
well conditioned girl, 18, with nothing but her life
ahead of her, completely in tune with her body, swimming
laps... And as it comes to all of us, painfully aware of
the years passing, her own physical mortality, she starts
to cry... And we see that Benjamin, come to meet her, is
standing above her.

Looking at the young girl... looking at her...
understanding...

> BENJAMIN
> You might have got a few more
> years out of it but you chose to
> do something so special... and
> unique... that there was only a
> short window of time you could do
> it...So even if nothing ever
> happened ... you would still be
> right here where you are now...

She's quiet... she knows what he's saying is true...

> DAISY
> I just don't like getting old.
> There's too much chlorine in here.

She turns to get out of the pool

232   EXT. LAKE PONTCHARTRAIN, LOUISIANA - DAYBREAK, 1964   232

Benjamin, Daisy holding onto him, riding the old
motorcycle along the lake...

233   EXT. THE DOCK AT THE LAKE - DAYBREAK, 1964   233

Benjamin walks out of the house wrapped in a quilt
carrying 2 cups of coffee.

Daisy sits in the familiar deck chair his father had sat
in looking out at the lake... Benjamin brings her a cup
of coffee... He sits beside her...

(CONTINUED)

                         DAISY
          I promise you, I'll never lose
          myself to self-pity again...

And as they watch the day begin...

                    BENJAMIN BUTTON'S (V.O.)
          And I think, right there and then,
          she realized none of us is perfect
          forever.

234   OMITTED   **234**

235   INT. A DANCE STUDIO, NEW ORLEANS - DAY, 1967   **235**

A small dance studio... a scratchy phonograph record
playing music... young girls learning how to dance...

And we see Daisy, in a long skirt over a long sleeved
leotard... wearing slippers... The first time we've seen
her dressed like this in many a year... happily teaching
young girls how to dance...

236   INT. DANCE STUDIO, NEW ORLEANS - NIGHT, 1967   **236**

We see Daisy alone... cleaning up... and for a brief
moment she stops, and dances... the smallest, most
tentative of steps... she sees in the studio's mirrors
Benjamin's been silently watching her...she spins and
grabs her knee in pain.

                         BENJAMIN
          You certainly are beautiful to
          watch...

She looks at herself in the dance mirror... just what
happens...

                         DAISY
          Dancing is all about the line....
          the line of your body...Sooner or
          later... you lose the line... you
          can never get it back...

She looks at him.

                                              (CONTINUED)

> DAISY (CONT'D)
> I figure you were born in 1918...
> 49 years ago... I'm 43... we're
> almost the same age... we're
> meeting in the middle...

And what she doesn't say, what they both know, is she's
going one way and he's going the other...Benjamin
affectionately...

> BENJAMIN
> (smiles)
> We finally caught up with each
> other...

She smiles, starts to turn...He turns her so they can
look at themselves in the mirror.

> BENJAMIN (CONT'D)
> Wait...I want to remember us just
> as we are now.

They stay like that for a moment longer... She looks up
at him and lays her head on his shoulder.

> DAISY
> ... I'm pregnant...

They look at each other, she smiles, nodding "yes," it's
true. And deeply moved he takes her in his arms...
grateful...touching her face... holding her...

237   OMITTED   237

238   INT. A NEW ORLEANS STREETCAR -- DAY, 1967   238

Benjamin and Daisy riding a streetcar, talking...

> DAISY
> You know I'd swear the nurse
> slipped and said it was a boy.

As they ride Benjamin looks over watching a father
sitting with his daughter... Daisy notices his look...

> DAISY (CONT'D)
> But I think it's a girl.

EXT. A NEW ORLEANS DINER - LATE AT NIGHT, 1967

Benjamin and Daisy sitting at the window at one of the
booths...

INT. SAME NEW ORLEANS DINER - LATE AT NIGHT, 1967

Daisy with a hot Fudge sundae... Benjamin just some
coffee... They're quiet... And Daisy says...

> DAISY
> I know you're afraid.

> BENJAMIN
> I'm not hiding it.

> DAISY
> Okay. What's your worst fear?

> BENJAMIN
> A baby born like me?...

> DAISY
> Then we'll love it all the more...

> BENJAMIN
> Okay, then how can I be a father
> when I'm heading in the other
> direction? It's not fair to the
> child. I don't want to be
> anybody's burden.

> DAISY
> Sugar, we all end up in diapers. I
> am going to make this work... I
> want this, and I want it with
> you...

> BENJAMIN
> I want you to have everything you
> want, all of it. I'm just not sure
> how to reconcile this.

> DAISY
> Would you tell a blind man he
> couldn't have children? You will
> be a father for as long as you
> can. I know the consequences.
> (MORE)

(CONTINUED)

                              DAISY (CONT'D)
                    I've accepted that. Loving you is
                    worth everything to me. I have to
                    go pee.
                              (laughs)

He smiles... She gets up and goes to the restroom. He
sits with his thoughts... he stands to pay and he notices
a television's on... a news report... he hears...

                         A MAN'S VOICE (V.O.)
                         (on television)
                    The oldest woman to ever swim the
                    English Channel arrived here today
                    in Calais ... having made the swim
                    in thirty-four hours, twenty-two
                    minutes and fourteen seconds...
                    the sixty-eight year old Elizabeth
                    Abbott arrived at 5:38pm Greenwich
                    mean time, exhausted but happy...

And we see dear ELIZABETH ABBOTT, coming out of the
water, completing the English Channel swim.

                         REPORTER (O.S.)
                    Mrs. Abbott, how would you sum up
                    in words, this achievement.

                         ELIZABETH ABBOTT
                         (on television)
                    I suppose anything's possible.

And as she smiles, after a lifetime of waiting,
triumphant... And Benjamin smiles for her, and for
himself, too... where anything is possible... Daisy's
come beside him...

                         DAISY
                    You ready?

                         BENJAMIN
                    Yeah.

He takes her arm... and as they go outside, moving along
the street...

                         BENJAMIN BUTTON'S (V.O.)
                    In the spring, on a day like any
                    other...

INT. THEIR BEDROOM, SUBURBAN TOWNHOUSE - MORNING, 1968

We see Benjamin in the bathroom brushing his teeth, he
crosses to the bedroom, grabbing his keys and wallet. He
heads for the front door.

                    BENJAMIN
          I'll be back in an hour.

And there's the sound of something falling... and then...

                    BENJAMIN (CONT'D)
          Honey...

And he runs out of the room... to see Daisy, fallen,
sitting on the stairs...

A glass of milk spilled on the carpet... and blood on her
nightdress...

                    DAISY
          You've got to call an ambulance...
          the baby's coming.

He runs to a phone...

                    BENJAMIN
          Operator, I need an ambulance...
          2714 Napoleon.

                    DAISY
          The baby's coming...

He runs back down to Daisy.

242   INT. LIVING ROOM - SUBURBAN TOWNHOUSE - DAY 1968   242

Benjamin paces around the living room listening to the
sounds coming from the bedroom. He walks into the kitchen
and hears the hall door open.

Benjamin is waiting in the hallway, a Paramedic comes out
of the bedroom door followed by the Doctor.

                    BENJAMIN
          Is everything good?

                                             (CONTINUED)

                              THE YOUNG WOMAN DOCTOR
                    Everyone's fine. She's a perfectly
                    healthy baby girl...

                              BENJAMIN BUTTON'S (V.O.)
                    She gave birth to a 5 pound 5
                    ounce baby girl.

243   INT. THEIR BEDROOM - SUBURBAN TOWNHOUSE - DAY, 1968   243

We see, lying on Daisy's chest, is a newborn baby...
Benjamin, walks over to her...He touches Daisy's face
wiping away her tears. He turns his attention to the
baby.

                              BENJAMIN
                    Did you count the toes?

Daisy smiles at him.

                              BENJAMIN (CONT'D)
                    She's perfect.

And Benjamin moved, looks at this precious child of
his...

                              CAROLINE'S (V.O.)
                    We named her for my mother...
                    Caroline...

244   INT. HOSPITAL ROOM, NEW ORLEANS - MORNING, PRESENT   244

Caroline's stopped reading... motionless...

                              CAROLINE
                    This Benjamin was my father? And
                    this is how you tell me...?!

Caroline, upset, gets up...

                              CAROLINE (CONT'D)
                    Excuse me.

She leaves the room.

244A   INT. HOSPITAL CORRIDOR, NEW ORLEANS - DAY, PRESENT   244A

Caroline stands in the hall. She pulls out a cigarette,
lights it, and watches more news about the hurricane on
TV. The bustle of the hospital, the exigencies of life
going on about her. The Nurse comes out of a room, seeing
her...

                    NURSE
          Hey, I know it's hard. You can't
          smoke in here.

244B   INT. HOSPITAL ROOM, NEW ORLEANS - DAY, PRESENT   244B

Daisy seeing her come back in...

Caroline quietly takes up the "book"...

                    CAROLINE
          "You grew, as the doctor had
          promised, normal and healthy..."

245   INT. THEIR BEDROOM, SUBURBAN TOWNHOUSE, NEW ORLEANS -   245
NIGHT, 1969

The room's dark. We see Benjamin in bed, the baby
sleeping between him and Daisy... And as Benjamin watches
them sleep... his 51st year on this earth... 34 years
old... a young man... He looks at his baby... he looks at
Daisy... in her mid 40s... her hair's begun to gray...
her face begun to show the natural touches of age... His
stare awakens her... She looks at him sensing he's deeply
troubled... He shuts his eyes... she watches him sleep,
Daisy as troubled as he is... but for very different
reasons...

246   EXT. A PARK - NEW ORLEANS - DAY, 1969   246

Benjamin and Daisy sitting with Caroline while she plays
in a park's sand box...

                    BENJAMIN
          You're going to have to find a
          real father for her...

                    DAISY
          What are you talking about?

                                        (CONTINUED)

                                   BENJAMIN
She needs someone to grow old
with...

                                   DAISY
She'll learn to accept whatever
happens... She loves you...

                                   BENJAMIN
Honey, she needs a father not a
playmate.

                                   DAISY
Is it me?

                                   BENJAMIN
Of course not.

                                   DAISY
Is my age beginning to bother you?

                                   BENJAMIN
Of course not.

                                   DAISY
Is that what you are telling me?

                                   BENJAMIN
You can't raise the both of us.

                             BENJAMIN BUTTON'S (V.O.)
It was your first birthday. We
had a party for you... the house
was filled with children...

247   INT. SUBURBAN TOWNHOUSE - NEW ORLEANS - DAY, 1969   247

The birthday party. A cake with a big number "1" candle.
One-year-olds not having a clue.

Benjamin walks into the kitchen to open another bottle of
champagne.

                                 A FATHER
Before you turn around they'll be
in High School dating.

Benjamin manages a smile.

                                                (CONTINUED)

He looks at the age appropriate mothers and fathers with
their children...Daisy smiles at him and raises her
glass.

247A   OMITTED   **247A**

248   INT. SUBURBAN TOWNHOUSE - LATER IN THE DAY, 1969   **248**

The house is empty, the guests gone... Daisy busy
cleaning up from the party. She stops to look outside.
Benjamin is sitting on the curb... the baby, in her party
dress, sitting on his knee... As Daisy stands at the
window watching him with their baby...

249   INT. THEIR BEDROOM - SUBURBAN TOWNHOUSE - EARLY MORNING   **249**
           1969

Benjamin, dressed, watching Caroline in her crib, asleep.
Daisy in bed, asleep.

                    BENJAMIN BUTTON'S (V.O.)
               I sold the summer house on Lake
               Pontchartrain... I sold Button's
               Buttons... I sold the sailboat...
               I put it all into a savings
               account... And so that you and
               your mother could have a life, I
               left before you could ever
               remember me...

He stops to put a bank book on the night stand, along
with a house key... the sound of the key is just enough
for Daisy to stir. He starts to leave... He turns to
go... and he sees Daisy is looking at him... A look not
so much of anger, or hurt, not of resignation, but a look
of acceptance... that this is what her life is now... He
crosses out of the dark room silently closing the door
behind him...

250   EXT. SUBURBAN TOWNHOUSE, NEW ORLEANS - MORNING 1969   **250**

He starts the motorcycle, and with just the shirt on his
back he rides away...

251   INT. SUBURBAN TOWNHOUSE, NEW ORLEANS - MORNING 1969   251

Daisy still lying in bed, the sound of the motorcycle
driving away. She gets up and walks to the window and
watches him ride away.

252   INT. HOSPITAL ROOM, NEW ORLEANS - MORNING, PRESENT   252

Daisy, in her regal turban, propped up in her bed
silently looking out the window... the wind knocking
loudly again...

                    CAROLINE
              "I left with just the clothes on
              my back." I don't want to read
              this now. Can you just tell me
              where he went?

                    DAISY
              I don't really know.

Caroline sits down and turns a page in the diary. She
finds a group of postcards bundled together with a rubber
band. She takes one out and looks at it.

                    CAROLINE
              It's for me. 1970. I was two.
              "Happy Birthday, I wish I could
              have kissed you goodnight."
                    (reading another)
              They're all for me. "Five, I wish
              I could have taken you to your
              first day of school."
                    (reading on)
              "Six, I wish I could have been
              there to teach you to play piano."
                    (another one)
              "1981. 13. I wish I could have
              told you not to chase some boy. I
              wish I could have held you when
              you had a broken heart. I wish I
              could have been your father.
              Nothing I ever did will replace
              that."
                    (she looks at
                    another)
                    (MORE)

                                        (CONTINUED)

CAROLINE (CONT'D)
I guess he went to India."For what
it's worth..."

252A   AROUND THE WORLD   **252A**

And Benjamin's voice comes in ...while we see him in
various places all over the world, a montage, a film
within a film, of the road he's taken...

BENJAMIN BUTTON'S (V.O.)
...it's never too late, or in my
case too early, to be whoever you
want to be. There's no time limit.
Start whenever you want. You can
change or stay the same. There are
no rules to this thing. We can
make the best or the worst of it.
I hope you make the best of it. I
hope you see things that startle
you. I hope you feel things you
never felt before. I hope you meet
people who have a different point
of view. I hope you live a life
you're proud of, and if you're
not, I hope you have the courage
to start all over again.

252B   INT. THE HOSPITAL ROOM, NEW ORLEANS - DAY, PRESENT   **252B**

Caroline finishes reading...

CAROLINE
"...and start all over again."

DAISY
He'd been gone a long time...

253-262 OMITTED   **253-262**

263   INT. THE DANCE STUDIO, NEW ORLEANS - ANOTHER NIGHT, 1980   **263**

A record's playing piano music. Classes are done.
Parents taking their children. We see Daisy, in her long
skirt... helping pick up errant clothing, the jackets,
the sweaters... It takes us a moment to recognize her...

(CONTINUED)

in the some twelve years since we've last seen her, 56
now, her hair's cut short... and it's gone mostly gray...
and, although her age is on her face, she still has a
dancer's posture, her head held high... carrying herself
with grace... and one thing that will never change, are
her unforgettable blue eyes... We hear the door
opening... Daisy, busy gathering, saying her
goodnights... glances toward the door across the
studio... And she sees a young Man has come in, a young
man in his twenties... standing silently, a stranger,
standing by the door...

                    DAISY
          I'm sorry, we're closing.

Daisy, as she closes up the studio, makes her way toward
him, Daisy looks over, the young Man hasn't moved... the
studio has emptied... she walks toward him... he's
wearing worn trousers, a coat that's seen better days...

                    DAISY (CONT'D)
          Can I help you? Are you here to
          pick somebody up?

Coming closer....

She stops, realizing who it is...

                    DAISY (CONT'D)
          Why did you come back?

...and she's taken aback by his youth, we all are...
sixteen years younger... in his 20s now... it's at once
staggering and heartbreaking... what age can do... And
she realizes, at that very moment, he was right all
along...

She stares at him... just the piano music. And despite
the gulf of time... there's a terrible aching they have
for each other... and before they can say anything...

                    CAROLINE (O.S.)
          Mom, mom...

Caroline, 12, comes hurrying in...

                    CAROLINE (CONT'D)
          Are you ready yet?

                                        (CONTINUED)

Benjamin stares at her appearance... And Daisy, can't
help herself, and seeing Caroline, Daisy, overcome by it
all, starts to cry.

> CAROLINE (CONT'D)
> Mom, what's wrong?

> DAISY
> I was just hearing a very sad
> story about a mutual friend I
> hadn't seen for a very long
> time... Caroline this is
> Benjamin... you knew him when you
> were... just a baby...

Benjamin comes closer...

> CAROLINE
> Hi...

> BENJAMIN
> Hi...

He reaches, taking her hand... needing to touch her...

> A MAN'S   (V.O.)
> Hey...

And a Man 50s, wearing a suit and a tie, comes in...

> THE MAN
> I'm sorry... I thought you were
> done...

> DAISY
> This is a friend of my family's...
> Benjamin Button... this is my
> husband... Robert...

They shake hands...

> ROBERT
> How do you do?

> BENJAMIN
> Pleasure...

There's an awkward quiet...

(CONTINUED)

                              ROBERT
                    Well it was very nice to meet
                    you... We'll be in the car,
                    darling...

                              DAISY
                    Alright, I'm just locking up...

And Robert and Caroline go outside to wait for
her...Daisy crosses to lock the door.

                              BENJAMIN
                    Wow, she's beautiful...like her
                    mother... Does she dance?

                              DAISY
                    Not very well.

                              BENJAMIN
                    I guess that would be from my side
                    of things.

                              DAISY
                    She's a dear sweet girl... she
                    seems a little lost... then who
                    isn't at 12? There's a lot of her
                    that reminds me of you.

And she shuts off a set of the lights.

                              DAISY (CONT'D)
                    My husband. He's a widower... was
                    a widower... He's an incredibly
                    kind, bright, adventurous man...

Benjamin smiles.

                              DAISY (CONT'D)
                    He's been a terrific father...

                              BENJAMIN
                    Good.

... and for a moment they stand in the dark studio...
seeing who they are now...

                              DAISY
                    You are so much younger.

                                              (CONTINUED)

                         BENJAMIN
                    Only on the outside.

She looks at him, and after all these years... she now
understands completely...

                         DAISY
                    You were right. I couldn't have
                    been raising both of you. I'm not
                    that strong.

He's quiet. She walks past him....

                         DAISY (CONT'D)
                    Where are you staying? What are
                    you going to do?

                         BENJAMIN
                    I'm staying at the Pontchartrain
                    Hotel on the avenue. I don't know
                    what I'm going to do, but...

And it seems like they want to hold each other. But they
can't. It's still. Suddenly they hear an insistent car
horn.

                         DAISY
                    They are waiting...

He nods and follows her, going out.

264   EXT. A STREET, NEW ORLEANS - NIGHT, 1980   264

She stops to lock the door. She turns, getting into the
car... and leaves... Benjamin stands on the corner, hands
in his pockets, the car driving by him... and Daisy can't
help but look at him... and then the car's gone... and as
he crosses the street and walks off into the night...

265   INT. HOSPITAL ROOM, NEW ORLEANS - MORNING, PRESENT   265

                         CAROLINE
                    I remember that. That was him.

Daisy nods.

                                              (CONTINUED)

265 CONTINUED: 265

The lights flicker and Caroline looks towards the TV as
the giant storm moves towards New Orleans. A Nurse comes
in.

                    THE NURSE
          The hurricane's changed directions
          it's going to make landfall
          sometime soon.

                    CAROLINE
          Am I supposed to do something?

                    THE NURSE
          Arrangements are being made to
          move people but it's up to you.

                    CAROLINE
          No, no we're staying.

                    NURSE
          I'll let you know if anything
          changes.

She leaves hurriedly.

Caroline goes back to the book.

                    CAROLINE
          "That night while I was sitting
          and wondering why I came back at
          all... There was a knock at the
          door..."

266   INT. BENJAMIN'S HOTEL ROOM, NEW ORLEANS - NIGHT, 1980   266

He opens it...and Daisy's there. He's startled to see
her...

                    BENJAMIN
          Come in...

She comes inside...an awkward quiet...

                    BENJAMIN (CONT'D)
          Are you alright?

(CONTINUED)

                              DAISY
                    I'm sorry, I don't know what I'm
                    doing here...

It echoes how she's feeling being there...They stand not
knowing what to say...And Daisy says, sadly, touching his
face...

                              DAISY (CONT'D)
                    Nothing lasts.

                              BENJAMIN
                    I have never stopped loving you...

He puts his hands on her shoulders....

                              DAISY
                    Benjamin, I'm an old woman now.

And he pulls her to him. They embrace.

And he pulls away and starts removing her purse and coat
from her shoulders...

LATER

Benjamin sits on the bed. Daisy stands across the room
dressing. He watches her.

She finishes dressing, grabs her coat and her purse and
heads for the door.

                              BENJAMIN BUTTON
                    Goodnight Daisy.

Stopping at the door.

                              DAISY
                    Goodnight Benjamin.

She closes the door.

267   INT. BENJAMIN'S HOTEL ROOM, NEW ORLEANS - NIGHT, 1980   267

We see Benjamin standing at the window watching as Daisy
gets into a taxi... and Daisy turning... to look back...
what they both somehow know, is a last goodbye...

                    BENJAMIN BUTTON'S (V.O.)
                 And as I knew I would, I watched
                 her go...

...and as the taxi drives away...

268   INT. HOSPITAL ROOM, NEW ORLEANS - MORNING, PRESENT   268

Daisy lying silently in her bed looking out the window...
And we realize Caroline's stopped reading...

                    CAROLINE
                 That's the last thing he wrote...

Daisy's quiet... they both are, alone with their
thoughts...

The wind has picked up considerably, rattling the window
even harder...

                    DAISY
                 It was a long time after your
                 father passed... There was a
                 call...

269   INT. DAISY'S HOUSE, NEW ORLEANS - DAY, 1990   269

And we see Daisy in her bathrobe, in her sixties...
drinking a cup of coffee... the telephone rings...

                    DAISY
                 Hello?... Yes?... Speaking -- I'm
                 sorry, I don't understand.

269A   EXT. DAISY'S HOUSE - DAY - 1990   269A

We see Daisy getting into a cab.

270   INT. A TAXI, NEW ORLEANS - DAY, 1990   270

We see Daisy riding in the back of a taxi.

                                              (CONTINUED)

                         DAISY
                It's the corner house...

She looks outside, and we see up ahead of her, the Nolan
House standing like a monument to time...

271   EXT. NOLAN HOUSE - LATE - DAY, 1990   **271**

Daisy walks into the back yard. The house has fallen into
disrepair. A solitary old man sits. Out of habit she
goes to the back porch... to the kitchen... going
inside...

272   INT. NOLAN HOUSE - LATE DAY, 1990   **272**

She comes in the back door. Queenie's daughter, now in
her fifties herself, sees her come in and calls to her.

                    QUEENIE'S DAUGHTER
                Come on in.

She stands in the breakfast room, along with a plain Man
in a plain suit...

                         DAISY
                I'm Daisy Fuller...

The Man stands...

                       THE MAN
                I'm David Hernandez with the
                Orleans Parish department of Child
                Welfare Services. He was living in
                a condemned building... the police
                found this with him... this
                address...it's got your name in it
                a lot...

And he gives her the journal...

                    THE MAN (CONT'D)
                He's in very poor health... he was
                taken to the hospital... He
                doesn't seem to know who or where
                he is... He's very confused...

                                        (CONTINUED)

                         QUEENIE'S DAUGHTER
                    I was telling Mr. Hernandez that
                    Benjamin is one of us. If he
                    needs a place to stay... it's
                    alright... he can stay here...

And just then we hear a PIANO playing... as if it were
being played by a child... with no skill... banging as
much as anything... And Daisy follows the sound of the
piano into the parlor...

273   INT. PARLOR, NOLAN HOUSE - DAY, 1990   **273**

And she sees his back... just a boy of 12 now... hunched
over... trying to play the piano... trying to play the
tune the woman had taught to him...

                         DAISY
                    Benjamin.

He turns at the sound of her voice. There is no
indication he recognizes her at all.

                         DAISY (CONT'D)
                    You play beautifully.

She comes and touches his back... He shrinks from her
touch.

                         THE MAN
                    He doesn't seem to like to be
                    touched.

And while he tries to play...

                         THE MAN (CONT'D)
                    He goes in and out of states of
                    recognition. The doctors said if
                    they didn't know any better, he
                    has the beginnings of dementia...

Daisy's looking at the boy, who was once the man she
loved... who she still loves... She looks into his
eyes...

                         DAISY
                    Do you remember me? I'm Daisy.

                                        (CONTINUED)

He looks at her. No sense of recognition.

                    BENJAMIN AT TWELVE
          I'm Benjamin.

                    DAISY
          It's nice to meet you Benjamin.
          Would you mind if I sit with you?
          I would love to hear you play.

He doesn't say anything. She sits down beside him on the
piano bench. He stops to look at her.

                    BENJAMIN AT TWELVE
          Do I know you?

He looks at her eyes. She looks at him... And as she
sits with him on the piano bench... he tries to play...
Daisy and Benjamin, "together again..."

274   OMITTED   **274**

275   INT. BACK DOOR NOLAN HOUSE - MORNING, 1994   **275**

And we see Daisy enters the back door.

                    DAISY'S (V.O.)
          And every day I would stop by...
          and make sure he was
          comfortable...

She moves to the kitchen hearing the following: Benjamin,
just eight now... Queenie's daughter cleaning up after
breakfast.

                    BENJAMIN AT EIGHT
          I want some breakfast.

                    QUEENIE'S DAUGHTER
          You just ate breakfast.

                    BENJAMIN AT EIGHT
          No I didn't...

                    AN OLD WOMAN
          You just finished eating, Mr.
          Button.

                                        (CONTINUED)

                    BENJAMIN AT EIGHT
                Don't think I don't know what you
                are doing?

And like an eight year old, or an old man old with onset
Alzheimer's -- which makes him nearly a helpless child,
he starts to rage... throwing things...

                    BENJAMIN AT EIGHT (CONT'D)
                You are all fucking liars!

And just then Daisy comes into the kitchen. She sees him
raging.

                    QUEENIE'S DAUGHTER
                He doesn't believe he just had his
                breakfast.

                    DAISY
                Now, why don't we see if we can
                find something else for you to do.

And as she puts her arm around him, taking him out of the
room, understanding...

276   INT. BENJAMIN'S ROOM, NOLAN HOUSE - DAY   276

We see Daisy with Benjamin in his room on the second
floor of the old house... She's drying his hair...And
he's oddly lucid...more articulate than his age would
indicate...

                    BENJAMIN AT EIGHT
                I have a feeling there's a lot of
                things I can't remember...

                    DAISY
                Like what, sugar?

                    BENJAMIN AT EIGHT
                It's like there's this whole life
                I had and I can't remember what it
                was...

He's frustrated by it...Daisy looks into his face...

                                        (CONTINUED)

> DAISY
> It's okay... It's okay to forget
> things...

277   OMITTED   277

278   OMITTED   278

279   EXT. NOLAN HOUSE - NIGHT, 1997   279

And we see Daisy, in her seventies now, getting out of a
cab with all of her luggage, one of the caretakers
meeting her.

> DAISY'S (V.O.)
> He was 5 when I moved in... nearly
> the same age I was when I had met
> him...

280   INT. GRANDMA FULLER'S ROOM, NOLAN HOUSE - NIGHT, 1997   280

Daisy, unpacking her suitcase with Benjamin's help,
taking out an alarm clock, a quilt, some photographs...
The "Just So Book.." Her personal things... moving in...
Benjamin, playing with the alarm clock, making the alarm
go off... again, and again...

281   INT. BENJAMIN'S ROOM, NOLAN HOUSE - NIGHT, 1997   281

Benjamin and Daisy, lying on his bed reading from
Kipling's "Just So" stories to him...

> DAISY
> This is the picture of old Man
> Kangaroo at five in the afternoon,
> when he got his beautiful hind
> legs...

> DAISY'S (V.O.)
> The days passed...

281A   EXT. PORCH, NOLAN HOUSE - LATE DAY, 2002   281A

Daisy, sitting on the porch on a rocking chair. Benjamin,
just a baby now, some months old, sleeping in her lap...

282   EXT. NOLAN HOUSE - ANOTHER DAY, THE FALL, 2000   282

And we see Benjamin, just three or so now, holding
Daisy's hand, walking with her in some autumn leaves...

                  DAISY'S (V.O.)
           I watched as he forgot how to
           walk...

283   INT. NOLAN HOUSE - ANOTHER NIGHT, 2001   283

Benjamin almost two...in the front room...playing...
Daisy sitting on the sofa...

                  DAISY'S (V.O.)
           ...How to talk...

                  DAISY
           What's my name? I'm Daisy...Can
           you say Daisy?...

284-285 OMITTED   284-285

                  DAISY'S (V.O.)
           In 2002, they put a new clock in
           that train station...

286   INT. TRAIN STATION, NEW ORLEANS - DAY 2002   286

And we see a workman covering the old clock of "Mr.
Cake's"... now taken down.

We see the new clock, a digital clock, high on the
terminal wall running the right way... going forward...
and as the clock turns... people hurrying to their
destinations, living their lives...

                  DAISY'S (V.O.)
           And in the Spring of 2003

287   OMITTED   287

288   INT. BENJAMIN AND DAISY'S ROOM, NOLAN HOUSE - DAY, 2003 288

Shadows dapple the room. Daisy sitting in an old chair
in the middle of the room... with daylight streaming in
on her... holding Benjamin on her lap...

                          (CONTINUED)

a tiny thing now... nearly newborn... he can almost fit
in her two old hands...

>   DAISY'S (V.O.)
>   He looked at me...

And we see him looking up at her...

>   DAISY'S (V.O.) (CONT'D)
>   ...then he looked into my eyes...

And we see him looking into her eyes...

>   DAISY'S (V.O.) (CONT'D)
>   ...and I knew... he knew who I
>   was...

The baby staring into her blue eyes...

>   DAISY'S (V.O.) (CONT'D)
>   And then he closed his eyes as if
>   to go to sleep...

And we see his eyes flutter and softly close... forever.
And as he lays in his beloved Daisy's lap... completely
still...

289   INT. HOSPITAL ROOM. NEW ORLEANS - MORNING, PRESENT   289

The wind a full out hurricane.

>   CAROLINE
>   I wish I'd known him.

>   DAISY
>   Now you do.

The lights flicker. Stay out. A siren goes off.

>   CAROLINE
>   Mom, I think I should go see
>   what's going on.

Caroline leaves the room. Daisy looks out the window at
the storm.

>   DAISY
>   Goodnight Benjamin.

                                        (CONTINUED)

And she closes her eyes for the very last time... and
it's dark... where it's peaceful, even safe...

We see the bustling hospital, the panicked patients,
Doctors and Nurses in the path of the coming storm...and
we hear Benjamin's voice...

290-291 OMITTED   290-291

                              BENJAMIN BUTTON'S (V.O.)
                    "Some people are born to sit by a
                    river."

292   EXT. RIVER   292

       ...And we see just that... Mr. Oti sitting by his
       river...

                              BENJAMIN BUTTON'S (V.O.)
                    "Some get struck by lightning."

292A   EXT. SOMEWHERE   292A

       And we see just that... Mr. DAWS being struck by
       lightning again...

                              BENJAMIN BUTTON'S (V.O.)
                    "Some have an ear for music..."

293   INT. THE PARLOR   293

       And we see the unnamed older woman playing the piano...

                              BENJAMIN BUTTON'S (V.O.)
                    "Some are artists..."

294   EXT. TUGBOAT   294

       ...And we see Captain Mike... with his tattoos --
       standing on his tug...

                              BENJAMIN BUTTON'S (V.O.)
                    "Some swim..."

295   EXT. ENGLISH CHANNEL   295

        ...And we see Elizabeth Abbott doing just that...

                         BENJAMIN BUTTON'S (V.O.)
                 "Some know buttons..."

296   INT. BUTTON FACTORY, NEW ORLEANS   296

        ...We see Thomas Button holding a button in the palm of
        his hand...

                         BENJAMIN BUTTON'S (V.O.)
                 "Some know Shakespeare..."

297   INT. KITCHEN, NOLAN HOUSE, NEW ORLEANS   297

        ...Tizzy reciting Shakespeare...

                         BENJAMIN BUTTON'S (V.O.)
                 "Some are mothers..."

298   INT. NOLAN HOUSE, NEW ORLEANS   298

        ...Queenie pointing at him...

                         BENJAMIN BUTTON'S (V.O.)
                 "And some people dance..."

299   INT. THEATRE   299

        ...And we see Daisy dancing... forever young...

300   OMITTED   300

301   OMITTED   301

302   INT. STORAGE ROOM, TRAIN STATION, NEW ORLEANS - DAY   302

        A storage room. Old track signs. Old waiting room
        chairs. The discarded, and forgotten. And lying on its
        side under an old tarpaulin -- is "Mr. Cake's" clock...
        the angel still pushing the hands... running backwards...
        as water rushes in and begins flooding the room...

                                              FADE OUT:

CAST AND CREW CREDITS

PARAMOUNT PICTURES
and
WARNER BROS. PICTURES
Present

The Curious Case Of
BENJAMIN BUTTON

Directed by
DAVID FINCHER

Screenplay by
ERIC ROTH

Screen Story by
ERIC ROTH
and
ROBIN SWICORD

From the Short Story by
F. SCOTT FITZGERALD

Produced by
KATHLEEN KENNEDY
FRANK MARSHALL

Produced by
CEÁN CHAFFIN

Director of Photography
CLAUDIO MIRANDA

Production Designer
DONALD GRAHAM BURT

Edited by
KIRK BAXTER
ANGUS WALL

Costume Designer
JACQUELINE WEST

Music by
ALEXANDRE DESPLAT

Sound Designer
REN KLYCE

Casting by
LARAY MAYFIELD

BRAD PITT

CATE BLANCHETT

The Curious Case Of
BENJAMIN BUTTON

TARAJI P. HENSON

JULIA ORMOND

JASON FLEMYNG

MAHERSHALALHASHBAZ ALI

JARED HARRIS

ELIAS KOTEAS

PHYLLIS SOMERVILLE
and
TILDA SWINTON

A
KENNEDY/MARSHALL
Production

A
DAVID FINCHER
Film